MW00654973

HIRED KILLER

BISCAYNE BAY SERIES

BOOK 1

DEBORAH BROWN

HIRED KILLER
All Rights Reserved
Copyright © 2021 Deborah Brown

Cover: Natasha Brown

ISBN-13: 978-1-7334807-6-5

PRINTED IN THE UNITED STATES OF AMERICA

HIRED KILLER

Chapter One

I discreetly checked my watch. Right on time.

Grey Walker entered the coffee shop like he did every morning at this time. He scanned every inch of the interior as he moved up to the counter and placed his order. Whatever he said to the young barista, she giggled and blushed.

The man was enormous, well over six feet. He filled out his jeans, his biceps pushing against his t-shirt; not an inch of fat on his muscled frame. There was a sharp intelligence in his deep blue eyes.

Little did he know…

I waited impatiently for him to take his usual seat on the outside patio. The man was always aware of his surroundings, allowing nothing to happen that he didn't see.

I'd carefully chosen the red, knee-length, V-necked dress with the deep slit to show off my best assets and bronzed Florida tan.

He grabbed his drink and moved outside. For a man his size, he was understated and had the ability to fit in. I didn't want to be intrigued by this man, but it was too late for that.

I picked up my coffee, cold by now, and sucked in a deep breath to calm my jitters as I walked over. I needed to unleash the performance of a lifetime. "Is this seat taken?"

* * *

The occasional grunt cut through my reverie. I closed my eyes and let out a long sigh. Even though less than twenty-four hours had passed, my nerves had only calmed slightly. I turned and faced the man handcuffed to the bed behind me.

Grey's lashes fluttered. He cautiously looked around, and then his eyes snapped open. "What the devil?" he growled, jerking at the handcuff on his right wrist, the other end attached to the bedpost. He found it unforgiving, as evidenced by his wince. His blue eyes, frigid as the Atlantic, settled on me. "You…" He yanked hard and hissed. Despite the pain, he ratcheted up his futile attempt to get away.

I rounded the bed and slapped his forearm. "Stop before you bruise your wrist or, worse, scratch up my brass bedframe. It's an antique." I licked my finger and polished the finish.

His free arm flew out, fingers wrapping around the strands of my shoulder-length strawberry blond hair and forcing me face to face with him, our noses within a breath of touching. Those lips. So close. I'd had a fantasy or two about them already. I forced myself to maintain eye contact and keep my naughty thoughts in check.

"The last I remember, you came on to me at a coffee joint in Orlando. We talked, then walked out together. You tripped, and being a gentleman—most of the time, anyway—I offered to help you to your car and…" Grey looked around the room. Staring out the sliding pocket doors, he took in the view of the waters of Biscayne Bay. He tightened his hold.

"Ouch." To my surprise, he untangled his fingers giving one last tug on the ends of my hair. "This is the first time I've…"

"Kidnapped is the word you're looking for, and it's a felony," he said in a stern tone.

"You listen to me, Grey Walker." I matched his tone, not certain where to begin. *I saved your life* seemed a bit abrupt.

He snorted, cutting me off. "One of us is a nutjob, and it isn't me."

"That's not very nice." Although even I had to admit he had a point. "Would you like some water… anything?"

"What I'd like…" He jerked on his wrist and sucked in a breath. His annoyance increased, and he grabbed a fistful of my hair again and brought my lips crashing against his.

Oh, what the heck! If this was to be my only kiss, I wanted it to be a good one. The chemistry exploded between us as his lips moved over mine. I put everything into it and kissed him back.

Grey intensified the kiss and just as abruptly

jerked back, his face a riot of emotions, his dark hair stuck on end. I traced his morning scruff, and he sucked in a deep breath. "Ransom? What? Let's make a deal before I lose all feeling in my wrist."

I sat up. "You whine worse than a girl."

He lurched straight up and grabbed the back of my shirt. "You're not going anywhere until I find out what's going on."

The bedroom door flew open. In bounced Avery English, investment guru and one of my two best friends. I'd trust her with my life. She was in jeans, her bare feet sliding across the wood floor and brown hair swinging around her shoulders. Her glasses looked more ridiculous than usual. She collected frames, the uglier the better, even though she had perfect vision. "Cutie's awake. I'm impressed—he just got his eyes open, and you're doing it already," she said in admiration. "Guess you didn't overdo the drugs, since they appear to have already worn off."

I jerked out of Grey's grasp, scooted to the edge of the bed, and perched on the side, an arm's length away should Grey want to wrestle again.

"She drugged me?" Grey was talking more to himself than anyone else.

I absently patted his hand.

"Harper… if the rest of him looks this good…" Avery shifted to get a closer look, ogling every inch of Grey.

He took note of his bare chest and tugged the sheet from under his arms up to his chin.

"Behave yourself," I told Avery, my cheeks burning. I'd tell Grey later that I wasn't molesting him—I'd spilled water on his shirt while attempting to get him to take a drink.

"If you don't call the cops, you're an accessory," Grey told Avery, and despite the pain, as evidenced by his grimace, he jerked on his wrist again.

"Stop." I smacked his forearm.

Avery dropped the folder under her arm on the bedside table. "Got your new identity," she said to Grey.

"My what?"

"I haven't explained yet," I said weakly.

Avery smirked, obviously betting that explanations had flown out the window once we locked lips.

"So Nutjob, does this mean I'm getting out of here sometime soon?"

"That's so sweet, the two of you have special names already," Avery cooed. "That's a good one. Have you come up with a name for him yet?" I shook my head. "I'll help you figure out something fun."

The door opened again and Rella Cabot, CEO of the Cabot Family Foundation and my other bestie, marched in wearing one of her flawless suits. "I thought we agreed you wouldn't bring him *here.*" The angry blonde jabbed her finger at Grey. "Now, you're going to have to really kill him." She hadn't been on board with my plan from the beginning. *Get therapy and stop inviting trouble into your life,* she'd told me.

"Remember, the one thing that we did agree on was that I'm not a killer." My hand moved absently to rest on Grey's chest. I felt him stiffen under the sheet. "Nothing's changed, and I didn't have anywhere else to take him that wouldn't attract attention. I could hardly drag him into some seedy motel." I squirmed at the thought.

"Are you forgetting we have cameras in the elevator?" Rella's demanding tone hadn't diminished. "I'm fairly certain that you didn't drag his butt up the stairs."

Avery backed up and leaned against the arm of a chair. "Took care of it already." In addition to growing her client's portfolios, the math wizard had a long list of talents that included the manipulation of anything electronic.

"News flash: this man knows where we live, or will soon," Rella shouted. "Then we'll be the ones in handcuffs and headed to prison."

I rubbed my ear. "Rella, keep that up and you'll lose your voice."

The three of us had been good girls, rule followers, when we met at the University of Miami. Avery and I had recently embraced our inner wild child, but Rella happily continued to toe the line.

"I've got a plan to sneak him out of here the same way I got him in. I'll be needing your expertise again." I nodded to Avery, signaling that she needed to once again erase all trace from the security cameras. "But first, I need to tell him a few things." That the two of us could end up dead topped the list. I wanted to peek at Grey out of the corner of my eye, but stayed focused. It was more important to calm Rella's anger.

She tugged at a lock of hair that had dared to come lose from the bun at the nape of her neck. She always managed to maintain an impeccable appearance, even first thing in the morning. "We all agreed," she reminded me. "You need to live up to your part. Keep your word."

She'd warned me—*This plan of yours is craziness. Don't do it. You could end up in jail or, worse, dead*—and I knew she thought she'd gotten a promise out of me, but I had to see this plan of mine through.

I nodded despite wanting to ask for another meeting so I could plead my case and convince my friends that this was the right-ish course of action.

Rella kicked off her stilettos, hooked them over her finger, smoothed her skirt, and strode out the door.

"You know how Rella is," Avery consoled me. "She follows a plan and never deviates. I have faith that you won't put us in danger. If you need me for anything, you know where to find me."

"Once I explain everything to Grey…" I still wouldn't want him to leave. Instant attraction, the kind I'd always scoffed at, had bit me big time.

Avery nodded, and with a quick wave, she left, running to catch up to Rella.

Grey shifted. I could feel his heat at my back. I took a deep breath, working up the courage to start talking.

Grey broke the uneasy silence. "I'll take that water."

I reached for the unopened bottle I always kept on the nightstand, unscrewed the cap, and handed it to him, watching as he downed it. "Avery called you cute. You're actually hot. 'Cute' doesn't do you justice."

"Flattery, huh?" Grey handed me back the empty bottle with a smile. "Can't wait to hear what you have to tell me. I'm betting it's a doozy."

"You're taking this calmly."

"Going on instinct. I discarded the idea of you being a serial killer early on. I'm banking on not being wrong and that I get to walk out of here with my parts intact."

"I promise you'll be leaving in one piece." I smiled tentatively. "Where to start?"

"The beginning." He rolled his shoulder.

I pushed him on his back and straddled him, cuffing his free wrist to mine. Then I unlocked the other cuff and rubbed his shoulder. I didn't miss the grin that appeared for a half-second. And it didn't escape my notice that he hadn't fought me off. I rolled over and lay next to him, sharing the same pillow, sucked in a deep breath, and blurted out, "Someone wants you dead, and it's not me."

Chapter Two

"Two weeks ago, I stopped by a… shared office space." I knew Grey noticed my hesitation, but I wasn't ready to involve another person at this point. "One of the phones wouldn't stop ringing. I answered, thinking I knew who was on the other end." My dad. A story for another time. "I knew that even if I was wrong, the phone was running a voice-distorting app, so the other person wouldn't know who really answered."

"What you're saying is that it wasn't your phone. Then whose was it?"

"Heron?" the man had boomed through the receiver.

I didn't bother to enlighten him that it was the first I was hearing the name.

"Got a job for you. Grey Walker, an ex-cop out of Orlando, needs to die — the sooner the better. It's my understanding you require half up front. I'll wire it as soon as we hang up."

I stood, gaping at the phone until he barked, "You there?"

"Send the contact information," I answered, still trying to wrap my mind around what he was asking.

"You f— this up and you're dead. Time's running out."

I was left staring at a dead line.

I ignored Grey's question. "The man on the phone wanted you dead. If I didn't take the job, he'd hire someone else who'd probably kill us both for good measure."

"I hate to break it to you, but I'm not dead. So now what?" Grey demanded. "Once your client figures it out, you're going to have to come up with a way to save your own ass."

"Well…" I hedged as his brows rose. "You kind of are. Your body's been transported to the coroner's office, and your nephew's been notified."

"I don't have a nephew."

"I thought about hopping on Craigslist and hiring a fake relative but had second thoughts. Then I remembered this acquaintance who'd told me anytime I needed anything, I could call and he'd handle it."

"I'm glad you didn't go with your first idea…" Grey shook his head. "There are some jobs where you shouldn't cut corners."

I wanted to roll my eyes but restrained myself. "Cut me some slack. This job was a bunch of firsts for me, and I had to improvise."

"Why not just off me and be done with it?"

"Because I'm not a killer or, as it turns out, a thief."

"Nobody mentioned thieves." Grey cast me a sideways glance.

"Another long story." I sighed. "My first

inclination was to sit you down and explain the situation, but I figured you'd write me off as a crazy person. I didn't have any proof. Then I got another call, more threatening, telling me my time was up. You know how my next bright idea worked out—here you are."

"Except that your story implodes when the coroner does a DNA test."

"Turns out your nephew has a friend in the coroner's office. The timing was perfect. A homeless fellow was brought in, and your ID found its way into his pocket. Identification from a family member will seal the deal. It should make the news sometime today."

"How did I die? Let me guess, the headline will be 'dirty cop dies in the street, gets what's coming to him,'" Grey said in a disgusted tone.

"OD'd in an alley."

"Damn." Grey winced. "Poor bastard."

"After the first call, while I was trying to figure out what to do next, I researched your background and think you got a rotten deal."

"You're in the minority. Even though nothing tied me to that woman's murder, her friends and some of my colleagues still thought I was a piece of… Fourteen years on the police force, and I felt forced to resign at thirty-four, since most of my co-workers made it clear they no longer wanted to work with me. Now this."

I reached across and clasped his free hand.

Gray huffed out an enormous frustrated

breath. "You have any clue who wanted me dead so bad?"

"I thought we could figure that out together." I ignored his snort. "The caller was willing to pony up two million dollars for your demise."

Grey whistled. "What makes you think he'll pay?"

"Please." I smirked, which made Grey grin. "I got half up front, which I've deposited in your new account, Steve."

"That's the best you could come up with? Let me guess… Steve Smith?"

"You know it's perfect, smarty; there's a jillion of them." Grey laughed, and I hoped I could make him do that more often. "Your other option is to step up and admit that the dead dude was misidentified, but that could very well be your ticket to the morgue, since you'd still have a target on your back."

His blue eyes flickered over to the bedside table. "Is my new life in that folder?"

I attempted to reach it and fell short. Grey wrapped his arm around my middle, and we rolled onto our sides. I grabbed it, he rolled us back to our former position, and I set it on his stomach. "There's identification. Two bank accounts set up in your name, one of them local, the other in the Cayman Islands. After your funeral, your nephew will go pack up your apartment. I haven't asked for that favor yet, but I don't anticipate a problem."

"Is this paragon your boyfriend?" Grey growled.

"I don't have a boyfriend. Good thing, too, as it keeps me from having to explain to another guy why I'm cuffed to you in the middle of my bed."

Grey chuckled and opened the folder, flicking through the paperwork. "This Steve fellow is impressive on paper." We lay there in silence while he read the documents. "For someone so young, you certainly have a lot of talents, and some of them could get you a lot of jail time."

"I'm only five years younger than you, but I'll admit that in the last year, I shed my 'goody two shoes' image and went wild for a short time. I figured out fairly quickly that I didn't enjoy the illegal side of life. You were my last job. I've retired."

"Have you decided what you're going to do with me?"

"That depends on you." I wanted to say *I'd like to keep you*, but that would only add to my *nutjob* impression. "I'm offering to help you figure out who wants you dead."

"Thank you. Again. For not offing me." Grey turned and faced me. "I'd like food and a shower. Not sure how we handle this." He raised our cuffed wrists.

"Will you promise that when you're ready to leave, you'll let me get you out of here without being seen?"

"I'm thinking I should stay for a day or two, since I have no clue what comes next and need to figure something out. You ready for that?"

I couldn't contain my stupid grin. "No problem. This is my condo, and I'll let my friends know you'll be here. Decide what you want to eat, and while you're in the shower, I'll have it delivered."

Grey wrapped a lock of my hair around his finger and looked out the sliding door. "That's a pretty amazing view for Orlando."

"I relocated you to Miami."

"Did I enjoy the ride?"

Grey was handling having his life upended pretty well. I ran my finger across his jaw. "A few more days' growth of facial hair, a pair of dark glasses, and a baseball cap, and you won't stand out as the old you."

"Your friends aren't going to be happy."

"If you reassure them that you're not going to call the cops the first chance you get and have them hauled out of here and jailed for having the bad sense to keep me as a friend despite my poor decisions, they'll lighten up."

"Just so you know, I'd never hang you out to dry," Grey reassured me. "Or your friends. I haven't had a chance to think about what I would've done in your shoes, but given time, I'll get there. I have a healthy sense of self-preservation, and I won't be doing anything to put myself in jeopardy."

"You're taking this a lot better than I would. You were cranky at first, but you got over it fast." I grinned. "This is one of those good news, bad news situations. I'm not sure what I'd do in your shoes." I took the key to the cuffs out of the pocket of my jeans.

"If I'd known where they were…" Grey waggled his brows.

I unlocked the cuffs and held out my hand. "Harper Finn."

Chapter Three

When Grey came out of the bathroom, he'd changed into the oversized cream bathrobe I'd left hanging on a hook. Tied around his waist, it barely covered him, showing off his tanned arms and legs. His black hair was wet and slicked back. He moved deftly across the room and pushed open the sliding doors, crossing to the railing and sucking in a lungful of air as he stared down at the blue waters of the Atlantic.

In a way, it felt like we were friends enjoying each other's company, but the reality was... I kidnapped him. Even though he was free to go, his life had been ripped out from under him. If he chose, a new one was within arm's reach, but it was scary nonetheless.

He stepped around the cushioned chaises and chairs and walked slowly from one end of the balcony to the other. He peered back over his shoulder through the windows, checking out the living room, dining room, and kitchen as he passed. Every room with a view of Biscayne Bay.

I pushed open the slider to the kitchen, waving him inside. "Hope you like coffee." I handed him a mug.

He took a drink and nodded as he checked out the dark wood kitchen cabinets and quartz countertops uncluttered by anything except a coffeemaker. "Amazing digs you've got here. My place is a hole in comparison—the only place I could find where management didn't watch television and already know my name." He downed the rest of his coffee and took in the view from a different direction while refilling it. "I saw my briefcase on the dining table. Not sure how you got it out of my SUV, but I appreciate it."

"Oh officer, I'm certain you've heard of a slim jim."

"You're a crafty woman," Grey said with a shake of his head, his lips quirking with amusement. "I've always avoided crazy women, but I'm thinking I shouldn't have been so hasty. I'm betting you have a good story, as well as a few more tricks up your sleeve."

"It's a long one. I'll tell you mine if you tell me yours."

Grey laughed and stalked towards me, wrapping his arms around me in a hard hug. "While in the shower under those amazing heads of yours, I gave thought to leaving; I'm not much for freeloading."

"Besides needing time to adjust… Unless you're going to disappear, to another country perhaps, you're going to need help to figure out who wants you dead. Besides, you're welcome to stay here."

"Not to be rude, but I'll need someone with a little more muscle for backup. Even you have to agree we can't just shoot anyone who gives us a problem." He laughed.

I threw a body shot, sweeping his legs out from under him and dropping him to the floor. His loud grunt and look of surprise assuaged my ego. "In addition to lifting weights, I kickbox."

"I should've heeded the warning the second your gorgeous green eyes turned frigid." He fisted my shirt and pulled me down to the floor, nose to nose with him.

A long minute passed with neither of us saying anything.

Finally, Grey broke the silence. "Running from an anonymous threat isn't much of a life. If the person who paid to make sure I'm dead finds out I'm not, you'll be the next target. I'm not leaving you unprotected."

"Stay here, pick my brain, and use those cop skills of yours to get this case solved." Grey didn't appear convinced. "Here's our first clue: the down payment was sent from an account in the Turks and Caicos to my account in the Caymans." Not mine, but I hadn't divulged that part of the story yet. "An attempt was made to snatch it back, but I had the foresight to have the money moved the second it landed."

A banging on the front door interrupted us.

"It's one or both of my neighbors. I'm

surprised they're knocking, since we all have keys," I'd barely finished telling him when Rella stormed into the room.

Grey jumped up and extended a hand to me.

"He's still here, and now he's not cuffed," Rella hissed, taking in the two of us bounding up off floor with disdain.

Avery ran in behind her, skidding to a stop on the wood floor. "I better not have missed anything." She appeared more nerdy than usual, in a pair of round wire-rimmed glasses that covered half her face, her hair disheveled, as though she'd fallen out of bed and hadn't bothered with a brush. It amused her to play the role she'd been assigned over the years by people who didn't bother to get to know her. In my assessment, she intimidated the hell out of most people, and it didn't help that the more they talked down to her, the more she doubled down to win the game. "Look at him, all hunky in that bathrobe." She ran her topaz eyes over him from head to toe.

Rella crossed her arms, steam practically coming out of her ears. "When are you getting him out of here?"

"I'm hoping he can stay for a few days. If you're adamant, then I'll move him out later today."

Grey tucked me against his side in a protective gesture. "I promise I'm not going to repeat a word of what's happened. Not that anyone would believe such a story."

I blushed.

"I'm not repaying Harper like that. Besides, she just convinced me I need her by my side."

"I bet she did." Rella huffed. "It's not a good sign when dreamy here calls you a nutjob and it's an apt description."

"So you think he's cute." I tried not to smile at her groan.

Grey grinned.

Avery laughed. For someone who claimed to be averse to drama, she somehow managed to always end up in the middle of anything going down, soaking it up with obvious glee.

"I don't want to come between friends, so I'll get dressed and leave." Grey's raised eyebrows asked Rella, *Is that okay with you?*

"Then I'm going with you." I fisted the sleeve of the bathrobe. "You're going to need someone to sneak around on your behalf, and who better, since I've been honing my skills of late? Another perk: I've got a friend or two who're always willing do something for a buck."

"That's a terrible idea." Rella turned on Grey, hands on her hips. "You need to tell Harper just that and, while you're at it, tell her to stay far away from you."

Avery hooked her arm through Rella's. "Give us a minute." She pulled her friend back out the door, and it closed with a click.

"Rella's right, you know. I'm not a safe person

to be seen with at the moment."

Grey was right, but I didn't want to admit it. "I say wait to see how the news plays your demise... and then there's your funeral."

"A splashy affair?"

I caught his almost-smirk. "I'm thinking something low-key."

The door opened, and the two women stepped back inside, presenting a united front. "Fine," Rella said with a huff. "You screw any of us and you die. I can promise it'll be gruesome." Her ferocity had me smiling at her. The woman had never hurt anyone in her life, but I had no doubt that if Grey turned on us, he'd be her first.

I rushed across the room and hugged her, pulling Avery into a three-way. "Thank you both."

"Neither of you are to go wandering around," Avery said. "If you need something that can't be delivered, I'll pick it up. Can't imagine what that would be."

"I'm not sure what help I can be, but know this: Avery and I have Harper's back." Rella turned and left.

Avery flashed me a secret smile of support and followed Rella out.

"I'm jealous. I've never known the kind of friendship you have with those two. I thought I did, but when my life hit the fan, everything changed. My partner had my back through the ordeal, but then we just lost touch." He looked down at the robe. "I should change."

"Since we missed breakfast, I ordered taco platters. They should be here soon." I held out my hand. "We have time for a quick tour of the rooms you haven't seen." I led him down the hallway of the shotgun-style condo—all the rooms on one side—and back to the master, pointing out the seldom used office, guest bathroom, and second master. "Make yourself at home."

Grey's eyes went to the sliders. "How high up are you?"

"Forty-second floor. We're at the tip of South Beach, and the turquoise water you see lapping the white sand is part of Biscayne Bay."

"Love the water, and even if I didn't, I'd want to stand here and soak it in."

"Believe me, I don't take it for granted."

The front door banged open. "Food's here," Avery yelled.

"I had it delivered to her unit," I answered his raised eyebrows. "Meet you in the kitchen."

Chapter Four

I took the bags that Avery had left and spread the food out on the small square island, grabbing plates and silverware and pulling out the woven-backed barstools with comfortable cushions. Having no clue what Grey liked to drink, I'd let him make his own choice. I heard his feet on the tile floor and turned as he came up behind me dressed in his own clothes—jeans and his now-dry t-shirt, which accentuated his muscled chest.

"Smells great." He surveyed the countertop and set down the folder I'd given him earlier.

"Before you sit your tuchus down..." I pointed to the oversized refrigerator, which I kept stocked with a variety of cold drinks.

Grey took his time scanning the shelves, deciding on a bottle of craft beer. I'd already chosen iced tea. "Something tells me you're out of my league." He slid onto the stool next to me. "Bring me up to speed on how to access my assets so I don't turn into a mooch."

I took a bite of my taco and moaned. "The mambo taco platter isn't going to break the bank."

"Our love of Mexican food is proof we're meant for each other." Grey grinned.

We sat in comfortable silence as we ate. I urged him to help himself and got up to fetch him another beer. When we were finished, we cleared the dishes and put them in the dishwasher.

I heard my phone ring, signaling an email alert. "Let's move into the living room. It's much more comfortable. My laptop's on the table, and I can find out if the message that just came in is life-altering." We settled on the cushy couch and shared the oversized ottoman. I opened my laptop. "Small wager: it's about you."

Grey laughed, conveying, *Not taking that bet.*

"You were positively ID'd as the unfortunate fellow found dead in the alley behind a liquor store." I turned it so he could read the screen.

"Now what?"

I turned it back toward me, opened another account, and read. "Your nephew had the body sent to a funeral home for cremation."

"What about the dead guy's family?"

"They were notified and declined to claim him, not wanting to shell out for the expense of a burial."

"Hope you've arranged a nice service."

"You better not be thinking about going," I admonished. "Too risky." I leaned over and opened the drawer in the glass end table, pulling out the remote. I flicked on the television, which hung on the side wall, turned to the "news all the time" station, and handed it to him. "If you're not a lead story now, you will be soon."

Grey grimaced.

I opened an email and found the contact information for the funeral home. "I suggested that your nephew choose a nice burial at sea, the Atlantic to be exact. Once the cops have released your apartment, he'll send one of his minions to clear it out, then head over to your office and do the same. They'll have both packed up in a jiff."

"My office is on my laptop. I'm certain that once the woman at the rent-a-desk place hears of my demise, she'll be pocketing the sticky notes and pens. I can't wait to meet this nephew of mine."

"Hmm… maybe not." I screwed up my nose. "Although he's impossible to miss if you run into him—built like an outhouse. Don't stare too long; he'll take that as an invitation to rearrange your face." At his raised eyebrows, I added, "Only repeating what he told me once."

"Can't wait to hear how you met this charmer." Grey's tone suggested otherwise. "My apartment came furnished, so it should only take a handful of boxes and an hour or two. Be nice if the cigars on my desk got packed… though I heard somewhere that they're not good for your health."

"You could resurrect your company under a different name."

"I hate starting over, and it looks like I'll be doing it again. This time, I think I'll be a figurehead and farm out the jobs."

"You're up." I pointed to the television.

Grey turned up the sound. "Bet these a-holes got a big laugh out of using an old photo where I was hungover."

I looked at the screen and back at him. "I'm partial to current you."

Grey glared at the television. "Hours after that photo was taken, I found out I was a person of interest in Mindy Graham's death. Internal Affairs converged on my desk and told me they had a few questions. It felt like a perp-walk in front of my colleagues, most of whom turned away. Since it was high profile, the news of my interrogation got out, and the media wouldn't let it go. Probably because there wasn't another viable suspect. I was told to take a leave of absence." Grey flicked off the television. "That newscaster was pompous. Not a scintilla of sympathy over my death. He focused his report on the scandal, not mentioning that there were never any charges. Made it sound like I got away with murder."

"Before stalking you, I read everything I could find about you and ended up with a few questions of my own. So this Mindy chick got the bright idea to fake her own death and frame you for her murder, then ended up dead for real. Why? Jilted lover? It wasn't clear in the reporting how long you and she dated."

"Dated?" Grey snorted. "We went out once, and it was an okay time. No reason to do it again. We had zero in common, which was evident by the end of the evening. I escorted her home, pecked her on the cheek, and was out of there. Three months later, her body was discovered by some neighborhood kids in a pond behind my house. In the preceding months, Mindy had told friends she was terrified of me. Right after the discovery, one of her girlfriends went to the cops and filed a police report. That, of course, made the news, which took it as fact without checking it out. They felt it should be given the same weight as if Mindy filed it herself."

"Did your lawyer question the girlfriend?"

Grey shook his head in disgust. "Cathy Silver, the woman who filed the report, told the authorities that I began harassing Mindy after our dinner. She didn't even have the right date or restaurant. I could understand if I'd been a bastard to the woman, but that wasn't the case. It truly was an unremarkable evening. Shortly after the date with Mindy, I met someone else. We hit it off, and I thought we were building something. Then it hit the news that I was a person of interest. Still don't know who tipped off the press. I called my girlfriend to explain, but her phone went to voicemail, and then the number was changed. Considering everything that was happening at the time, I took the not-so-subtle hint not to bother her. Shortly after, I heard she moved."

"Eventually you were cleared as a suspect in Mindy's murder?"

"No charges were filed. Not the same thing in my opinion. It was never made public that I'd been cleared, and it left people thinking I'd done it and gotten away with it."

"I read that Mindy left a journal detailing how she planned to set you up. Is that true?"

"It was her intention to plant blood evidence and personal belongings—not sure how she was going to get either one of them—and then move in with a friend out of state." Grey's snort left no doubt how stupid he thought that idea was. "Not everyone has a friend in the coroner's office, and her plan had enough holes that it would've imploded and she'd have found herself in legal trouble of her own."

"All over one crappy date?" I shook my head.

"I guess. I never understood it myself. I read what she wrote. There was excitement in her words. She was clearly caught up in her plan. Often wondered if there was something special about me that prompted the plan or if she'd have latched onto any poor schmuck who wandered into her path."

"You were a detective—did anyone stand out that you thought warranted a closer look?" I asked.

"There were a couple of Mindy's friends that I

would've questioned. I suggested it to my lawyer, and he flipped, told me to stand down and let the legal system handle it." Grey huffed out his annoyance. "Not long after I ceased to be a person of interest, the case went cold. Not that there were many leads to begin with. Shortly after, Mindy's father cornered me at the coffee house and told me I owed him for turning her journal over to the captain. That was when I learned he was the one who'd found it and handed it over."

"What did Mr. Graham want in exchange for his good deed?"

"He was adamant that I never mention his daughter's name again. I thought the way he worded it was a little odd, then realized his biggest fear was that I'd do a sit-down interview and drag the family through the mud. He didn't know me at all, and his attitude that I should be grateful made me want to punch him, but I sucked it up, reminding myself that he'd lost his daughter."

My first impulse was to hug him; I went for a knee pat instead. Dumb, I know. "You did get your job back?"

He nodded. "Because the union went to bat for me. It was suggested that it would be in the department's best interest if I resigned, as they feared never-ending news coverage, but I gave that suggestion the figurative finger and got assigned to desk duty. The atmosphere at the station was frigid, and I filled my do-nothing hours by setting up my investigation business. Got my PI license and rented desk space. On the couple of occasions that I had female clients, I hired the receptionist to sit in the room."

"I thought you were owed a public apology. Sorry you didn't get one."

"I stopped hoping for that to happen." Grey gave me a scrutinizing look. "I have a question or six of my own. Your story is that you'd been following me… for how long?"

"A little over a week." My cheeks flamed.

"You'd think I'd have noticed a beautiful woman hot on my tail."

"I disguised myself as a boy or an old woman and never went as myself except the day I arranged to meet you. That called for a short dress and heels." I relaxed at his smile. "I rehearsed a sexy walk and a stumble, hoping that you'd catch me before I hit the ground. You were every inch the gentleman, even helped me back to my car. That's when I stuck you with a needle."

"The stick only half-registered…" Grey paused, clearly wracking his brains. "Then nothing until I woke up in your bed. I'll admit to being more annoyed than scared, because you didn't strike me as a killer… unless my instincts had totally gone to hell."

Chapter Five

"You have an unfair advantage over me." Grey's eyes bored into mine. "You know everything about me, my underwear size included." He traced his finger down my burning cheek.

I mumbled incoherently, not wanting to confess that the more I'd researched, the more I wanted to meet him. "What do you want to know?"

"Everything." He chuckled as my cheeks burned brighter. "How did you meet your friends? What trouble were you getting into before you thought it would be a good idea to accept a job as a hired killer?" Noticing my hesitation, he said sternly, "If you need me to play hardball with you, I can tie you to the bed and tickle you to death."

"The three of us met in college. We were on the same floor in the dorm. We bonded over being labeled nerdy and uninteresting."

"Dumb kids." He snorted. "I'm assuming you majored in something non-criminal."

"Business and Art History. My dad thought the latter was a waste of time and money but was appeased by my bachelor's in business. Figured I could get a job if I made an effort." I remembered his proud face at graduation and smiled. "The first thing I did was start my own company — Finn Media. I'm a social media marketer, managing accounts for those who have no clue or are too busy. It's grown to six employees. No worries, though; as harried as my schedule gets, I can always make time for trouble."

"When I get back on track, I'll be one of your clients with no clue. Can't wait to see your office. It says a lot about a person."

"First door on the right." I waved in the direction of the hallway. "All my employees work from home, and that includes me. I'm up at the crack of dawn and video conferencing. Any emergency that comes up, I'm available, usually within minutes."

Grey looked around the living room, the sliding doors open to the balcony. "Thanks to you, I'm going to use this second chance to be less grouchy and enjoy every damn minute of life. But go on, I want to hear the rest."

"My company does well, but this condo was made possible by my granddaddy. He invested heavily in an unknown company called Microsoft. I'm sure you've heard of it." I laughed, remembering the shock that reverberated through the family when the will was read. "He divided it between Gram and my mom, and she left her share to me in a trust fund."

"Successful company? Trust fund? How is it you made the leap into criminal activity? Should be interesting," he mumbled.

"If I were to confess all my transgressions, it would wipe that indulgent smile off your face."

"If you're worried I'm going to turn you over for prosecution, I'm not. However, going forward, I'll be doing my best to talk you out of anything that could end in your arrest. But just so you know, I'm not going to get judgmental." Grey assured me. "I've had enough of it to last me a lifetime."

"Stole the same car twice—a two-million-dollar Bugatti." I whooshed out a breath. "That job came from another phone call that I should've let go to voicemail." At his raised eyebrows, I quickly added, "After an attack of conscience, I stole it back and parked it in the owner's driveway. I donated the money."

"I remember that case." Grey laughed. "You're a clever little thing. You were caught on surveillance from several different angles, and it frustrated law enforcement that they couldn't get a good description of the thief and put him behind bars. Pricey auto—you'd have gotten the high end when it came to sentencing. Surprised your contact on that job didn't burn up your phone again when it went missing. Another burner, I assume?"

I nodded. "If you need a phone, I have a box full. As for the client, I smashed the phone; didn't want it traced back to me if they sniffed a double cross."

"There's a missing piece of the story — the ringing phones, who do they belong to? You told me that the caller had no clue who they were dealing with, so who did they think they were talking to?"

"When my dad suddenly went missing more than a month ago, I went to his office and discovered that he was involved in more than one shady deal. Instead of minding my own business, which I'm not known for, a part of me thought I might find answers as to where he might've gone."

"Killer? Thief?" Grey asked.

"Honestly, I'm not exactly sure what he was doing. I do know that he had his hand in several criminal endeavors."

"Your mother? How did she handle it?"

"It's an age-old story — they dated, broke up, and she discovered she was pregnant. If you're going to ask if she tracked him down, the answer is no, and I don't know why. My mom died of cancer when I was ten, and I went to live with Gram. After a couple of years, Gram was diagnosed with some health issues and contacted my dad. Informed him that he had a daughter and needed to step up. I overheard her say, 'Sorry it's taken so long to notify you, but you need to get your ass here, before I croak and Harper ends up who knows where.' Her idea to contact him; nothing more than a wild hair."

"Is she…" Grey paused.

"No, her medical issues were easily treatable. Drama queen decided that she wasn't getting any younger and wanted to move to a Jimmy Buffet old folks' home with a couple of her friends, so she concocted a plan to provide me with a stable life." Grey laughed, which made me smile at him. "I wrestled a promise out of Gram that she wouldn't skate out of the area to enjoy her golden years, so she's not far up the coast. Gram, Dad, and I lived together for a short time so Gram could put Dad through the hoops, make sure he was suitable. It didn't take long for him to get wise to her machinations and expedite her move."

"What you're saying is that instability runs in your family?"

I covered my face and took a deep breath. "Why aren't you out the door?" I asked through my fingers.

Grey pushed my hands down. "Not going anywhere. You're way too much fun."

"In my defense, I wasn't a rule-breaker growing up—always toed the line. I'll admit I've always had snooping tendencies, though. It didn't help that my dad was a secretive fellow, and when he caught on that his little bookworm was nosey as heck, he threatened to ship me off to boarding school. I boldly attempted to blackmail him, something I'd seen on a TV show.

He laughed. I'd missed the mark in coming off tough and menacing like the guy on the tube." I smiled at the memory of that showdown, knowing in retrospect that my dad enjoyed every minute. "The compromise: I'd stay out of his office and he'd teach me a few skills—so I'm good with a lockpick, can boost a car and kick ass, and I'm an excellent shot, even though I don't own a gun." At Grey's laugh, I added, "Almost forgot, check your pocket. I left you something when you weren't paying attention."

Grey reached in and pulled out his car key, holding it up. "What the devil?"

"Almost left pickpocket off my list of talents."

"I'm surprised your dad was willing to teach you those tricks, since not a one of them is legal." Grey shot me a pointed stare.

"A couple of them I learned on my own." I grinned at him. "I pinky promised that I would never do anything criminal with those talents. And here I am. He wouldn't be happy with me."

"You said your dad disappeared. Of his own accord?" Grey asked.

"Don't know. Dad was a private man, and rarely talked about his life outside the house. I wasn't sure why an insurance salesman needed to be so secretive, but he said his clients deserved his discretion. That explanation worked until I realized it was a crock."

Grey's lips quirked slightly.

"A month ago, he went to New York to meet

with a client and never came back. His phone went straight to voicemail at first. Now nothing. I filed a missing person's report, and the cop was sympathetic but treated me like a dumbass since I couldn't answer most of the questions about Dad's life."

"He probably figured your dad just walked off," Grey said.

"He wouldn't do that, which is one reason I picked his office apart. I needed to know that he was okay and wanted to bring him home. My contention is he's in hiding, and if I could ask why, my guess is he'd say, 'Not telling you is for your protection.'" I needed a break and stood. "A cold one?"

"Water's good. I don't want to get sauced for the rest of this conversation." Grey winked.

I crossed to the kitchen and walked around the island a couple of times to calm my nerves. Then I reached into the refrigerator and grabbed two waters, heading back to the living room and handing Grey a bottle.

He tipped his towards me. "Did your dad leave any clues behind?"

"I had long-standing instructions that should anything happen to him—though he wasn't specific on the 'anything'—I was to empty his safety deposit box. That's where I found the keys to an office building he owns." It had surprised me at the time about how organized he left everything. "This whole time, I thought he worked out of his home office, five floors down. Clearly a ruse. I knew he owned the office building, having been there once or twice, but thought he rented out all the floors. It was a surprise that he left instructions to destroy everything on the third floor."

"I'm willing to put big money on you not following those instructions," Grey said with a knowing smile. "And that you still haven't, even after giving everything you found a thorough inspection."

"The third floor held a lot of finds. The most interesting was a dozen or so phones, all plugged in and charged. While going through boxes of records, I discovered the bank account that I had the money for your contract wired into. I justified answering the phone that day by telling myself I could pretend my dad was still in business. It didn't take long to figure out that I was in way over my head. Eventually I took a sledgehammer to all the phones except the one. I'm awaiting notification—once the other million lands in the account, I'll toss that phone."

"Time to pay up now that I'm dead." Grey waggled his brows.

I opened the drawer in the side table, taking out the phone and checking the screen, then pocketing it. "Nothing yet. Thankfully, I'm not now and never will be dependent on illegal income." I stared out at the cloudless sky and the sun streaming through the doors.

"I'm thinking you're a person who needs to stay busy or you go looking for trouble. One thing we have in common—neither of us likes to sit and do nothing."

"I've been thinking…" I ignored his playful groan. "You've got investigative skills. We should partner up, and for your first case, you should figure out who wants you dead. After that, I'll hire you to help me find my dad. All you need is a little makeover, nothing drastic, and you can get out and mingle with no one the wiser."

"We'd have to work under the radar." He stared back at me, amusement in his eyes. "My current licenses are still valid, but should anyone question them, they'd trace back to a supposed dead man."

"ID under your new name is in the folder I handed you. You could cultivate clients that don't care how work gets done, as long as it does. It's rude to roll your eyes."

"Listen to me, young lady." Grey shook his finger. "No more loopholes or shortcuts for you. Going forward, you need to operate straight-up legal. Using fake ID is crossing that line."

"You may have to factor in some wiggle room." I waggled my brows. "Before we do anything, we should probably wait until after your funeral. Be respectful and all."

Chapter Six

Grey had fallen asleep on the couch for the second night in a row. Good thing it was comfortable, or the aches and pains would've taken their toll. It also eliminated the awkwardness of us being, after all, strangers. The television stayed on, sound muted; it didn't take long for the ex-cop's death to go from being the lead story to a brief mention, a boat explosion taking its place.

The following morning, we sat on the balcony, staring out at the water and finishing up our coffee. The ringing of my phone interrupted the silence, and we both moved back inside.

"You've been cremated," I said, hanging up the phone. "That was your dear nephew, updating me that the cops released your apartment and he had it cleaned out and made it look like everything had been hauled to the dump. For some reason, he thought that was a good idea. Your stuff is in a storage unit in Miami, and you have a month to pick up your stuff or cover the cost."

"My nephew's been a busy fellow. Is there going to be a service?"

"If anyone calls the funeral home inquiring, we'll also get that update." I stood and crossed my hands. "Dearly beloved… I'd be happy to say a few words."

"You're just full of tricks, aren't you?"

"I aim to please." I curtsied and plopped down next to him.

"My dear nephew… I seem to have forgotten his name."

"Sarcasm." I tsked.

"Said no one ever," Grey mumbled.

I needed a good stall, as I didn't want to name names or resort to the other option—lie. "I need to go to my dad's office. You want to ride along?" I was over being housebound and needed to soak up some sunshine.

"Nice try—ignoring my question and asking one of your own. It isn't going to work. I'm on the alert for that trick."

"Also thought that while we're out, we could hit up the storage unit and, depending on the number of boxes, make a trip or two back here. You're probably ready for a change of clothes."

Faster than a snake, Grey had me on my back and staring up into his pair of frosty eyes. "You've got two seconds before I unleash harsh interrogation techniques."

Maybe now wasn't the time to ask what that might entail. "Shark," I squeaked, knowing he'd be irked when he found out it was a name Ender no longer used.

"Jones Somebody would've been more believable." Grey grunted and tipped to the side. "Dammit, that hurts." He peered over his shoulder, then stretched out and lay still. "Get that cat off me. His claws are digging holes in my back."

My black Maine Coon, Mobster, had gone through a few names before I hit on one he responded to. He didn't care for visitors and took cover, hiding out until yesterday, when he introduced himself by jumping on the ottoman and biting Grey's big toe.

"Get down," I ordered, which had a slight chance of working. His yellow eyes stared back, letting me know that ordering him around wasn't going to work. Tactic two: "Want some food?" His twenty-five pounds leaped gracefully to the floor and darted to the kitchen. "Apparently he doesn't like it when you molest the woman who feeds him."

Grey sat up, pulled up his t-shirt, and turned his back to me. "Am I bleeding?"

"The blood's pouring out." I squinted and ran my fingers lightly over his skin. The claw marks were barely noticeable. "Fetch yourself a paper towel, and I'll do a mop-up when you get back from giving Mobster a treat. There's an open can of cat food in the refrigerator. Consider it a bonding moment with my feline—his affections can always be bought with tuna."

"Your empathy is overwhelming."

I attempted to roll away and was held in place by a muscled arm.

"When I'm done in the kitchen, we'll be off on our road trip."

"Tell Mobster he's a good boy; he likes that."

"Yeah, sure." Grey stood and helped me to my feet.

I made my way to my bedroom and disappeared into the bathroom. After a quick shower, I chose a hot pink A-line sleeveless tank dress and a pair of slide sandals. Standing in front of the mirror, I pulled my hair into a high ponytail. I took a wad of keys out of the armoire, grabbed my purse, and met Grey in the hallway. He'd pulled on a plain baseball hat that I'd found and left on the table.

"Am I incognito enough?" Grey stood in front of me in jeans and a t-shirt, his appearance disheveled and his beard more than a few days past a neat stubble.

I skirted past him and opened a drawer in the buffet table. "I've got these reflector sunglasses that aren't too girly. Between them and the hat, no one's going to recognize you, and if they do, they'll think, close resemblance, but not you." I held out the car keys, which he took, then grasped his hand in mine. "Stairs or elevator?"

Grey looked at me in amusement. "When was the last time you bolted down forty-two flights of stairs?"

"A little competition? First one to hit the

bottom gets to be bossy for the day."

Grey stared as though he could uncover my secrets. "No deal. I smell a setup. Elevator works for me."

I laughed as we let the door shut behind us, then stuck my security card in the panel next to the elevators, and the doors opened. "We have our own elevator for this floor."

Grey eyed the keys in his hand. "Where's my SUV?"

"In the garage, a car cover over it."

"I'm betting my 'nephew' can get it traded for another ride registered in a phony name." Grey stared at me like he thought it was a done deal. "And all of that is a crime."

"How about..." I smiled sweetly. "My company buys it, and if you get pulled over, then you decide which license to hand over."

He unleashed an irritated sigh. "I need to get this mess figured out so I can... that's a good one, I have no clue." He put his finger across my lips as the doors opened into the garage. "No apologizing. I know that's what you were about to do."

I led him over to the black Range Rover parked in front of his SUV.

He opened the door, helped me inside, and walked around, sliding behind the wheel. "Nice ride."

I programmed the GPS.

Grey headed out of the underground parking,

taking everything in as he pulled out onto the street. He slowed at the curb to stare up at the building. "Are all the units individually owned?"

"About ten percent are owned; the rest are rentals. The owner of the building is a friend and has been buying back the units as they come up for sale. It's in the contract for the unit I purchased that if I sell, it has to be back to the corporation and at market value." Rella had never publicly disclosed that she was the owner, and I wasn't doing it. "The building's got all the amenities and is well-maintained. There's a gym on the twenty-first floor; your card key will open the door." I reminded myself to give him one when we got back. "The property has beach access. Life doesn't get much better."

We cut over to the Causeway and past the islands where millionaires bought waterfront mansions, then down Highway One and over to a one-way street that was a straight shot to my dad's building, which sat just short of an Interstate underpass. Grey pulled into the parking lot on one side of the square four-story white stucco building, braking and craning his neck to check out the billboard that graced one side at the top, currently advertising a local brewery.

I followed his eyes. "My dad boasted that he had a waiting list for that ad space, which surprises me, since the majority of traffic is flying by on the freeway." A pickup parked in front of the glass entry doors on one side caught my attention. "Hmm... the building's empty, so that truck was either dumped or..." I didn't want to go borrowing trouble. "Either way, it doesn't belong here."

Grey passed it and backed into a space at the far end under a tree. We got out and checked out the interior of the truck as we headed for the door, seeing a few tools on the front seat. Grey, who was several steps ahead of me, turned and pushed me back. "Door's cracked. This is where you call the cops and have them check it out."

"No." I turned and ran back to the SUV, reaching under the driver's seat to retrieve my stun gun.

"Is that what I think it is?" He eyed it suspiciously.

I pulled the trigger, and it made a buzzing noise. "The battery's still good. You mess with me, buddy, and I'll lay your butt out on the asphalt."

Grey's lips twitched.

I wanted to smile, but knowing how controlled he was, he'd see it, know I was onto him, and stop with the almost-laughs.

Grey held out his hand. "I'll take that, before we have a dead body to dump."

"I'm corrupting you."

"It was a fast trip to the dark side, and since I don't show any inclination to end our association, I need to step up." I'd given Grey a burner phone, which he took out of his pocket and used to snap a picture of the truck's license plate.

I grinned. "You tell me what to do, and as long as it's not wait out here in the parking lot, I'll follow your instructions."

"You're going to do exactly what I tell you, as hard as that will be. I'm going to confront whoever that is and hope I don't find myself staring down the barrel of a gun."

I grabbed his arm. "I didn't think about real guns and bullets. Maybe you should go for a walk and I'll call the cops." Not paying attention to what I was doing, I stepped into the doorway, which elicited a growl from Grey. He lurched forward, arm out, and at the same moment, a wild-eyed twenty-something crashed into me, the box he was holding crashing to the ground.

The intruder righted himself and yelled, "Who the hell are you?" He pushed me back, and I landed hard against the wall.

Grey's fist made contact with his nose, and blood poured down the front of the man's shirt. The guy yelped and covered his face. Grey hauled him up by the back of his shirt, sent him spinning into the wall, and held him there. "What are you doing here? Start talking before I black both your eyes."

"Looking for small items to fence," he moaned, blood seeping between his fingers. "Didn't think anyone would be here."

Grey loosened his hold and shoved the guy to a sitting position on the ground. "Call the cops." He pointed to me.

I shot him a "we can't do that" stare. "I bet he won't come back. Will you?" I said to the man, who attempted to shake his head and fell back, groaning. "You by yourself?" I looked behind me at the open door to the stairwell.

Grey bent over and flicked through the contents of the box—burner phones and a cash box. I hadn't seen them before and wondered what floor they came from. Grey straightened, fisted the back of the man's shirt, and dragged him over to his truck. "I even see you in the neighborhood, and you're dead."

"I won't be back. Promise," the man muttered, stumbling to his feet. He hobbled into his truck and gunned it out of the space, over the sidewalk, and out on the road.

I bent down, picked up a lockpick, and held it up. "Now we know how he got inside."

"I take it this place doesn't have a security system?" Once inside, Grey kicked the door closed and tugged on the handle.

"Not sure why Dad didn't have one installed. Maybe he thought the insurance company sign on the side of the building would signal 'nothing to see here.' The business moved out before he bought the building."

"How about a tour?" Grey slung his arm around my shoulders.

"Through that door is an elevator, but it's locked. Needs servicing. The rest of the ground floor consists of a handful of parking spaces, the garage accessible from the rear of the building with a key card." I opened the door to the stairwell. "There's four floors. The top is an attic-like space and a dank hole because the billboard blocks the light to the handful of miniscule windows." I started up the stairs. "Last time I was here, I made a point of locking the doors to the various floors." I noted one door open a sliver. "We can assume that the intruder started with the first floor."

Grey stepped in front of me and shoved the door wide open. I poked my head around his shoulder; it was the same smelly mess it had been before. The previous tenant had thrown whatever they didn't want on the floor before moving out, then unplugged the refrigerator and left food inside to rot. It was my guess that they'd been asked to move and left the rotting mess as a one-finger salute.

Grey grumbled under his breath as he checked every corner of the wide-open space. He opened a couple of doors and, after a quick glance, stepped back. We moved to the second floor. It was locked.

I reached into his pocket while he stared, a smirk on his face, took out the keys and opened the door, then stepped back. Grey stepped inside and gave the space, identical to the floor below, a once-over. There wasn't any trash to step around, but it needed a good cleaning.

The third floor—another large, unimpressive space—was the one that my dad had occupied. He'd moved in an oversized wood desk and put it in front of the window. In addition to his chair, there was a pair of enormous leather chairs that showed signs of wear. A bookcase unit took up the entirety of one wall. What most people wouldn't know unless they owned one was that the middle section swung back, revealing a safe. It held bank records, guns, ammunition, cash, and more phones, the latter still in their original packaging. Another added feature—a drawer that ran the length of the unit and had been outfitted with plugs for charging electronics.

Grey checked out the space and crossed to the windows that ran from wall to wall. From this vantage point, you could see two different worlds—older office buildings and warehouses on one side of the freeway and towering high-rises once you cleared the underpass. "Interesting location. This building sitting empty is an invitation to thugs like the one who just left to come have a look around, see if they get lucky and find something. Or squatters."

"I don't know what happened to the other tenants, but at one time, all the floors were rented. I'm betting whatever kind of business my dad conducted, it didn't involve foot traffic." The more I uncovered about dear old Dad, the harder it was not to believe that he had a major hoodlum gig going. Unless the person who called in a hit on Grey was as mistaken in thinking my dad would carry it out as he was in my doing so. But I wasn't making any snap judgments until I talked to him. I hoped with everything in me that we'd see one another again, and not on visiting day at some jail.

Grey pulled me into his arms for a hug; he must've been reading my mind and figured out that's what I needed. After a moment, he stepped back and stared down at me. "I've got a proposition for you."

"First time and all? It's a little dirty in here for us to be..." I scissored my fingers. "Where's the romance?" I hadn't meant to utter the 'R' word out loud.

Grey laughed and shook his head. "You need a presence in this building to deter thieves. I'm thinking I'd be an ideal temporary tenant until your father comes back. I can discourage break-ins and send a message that it's now occupied. Another upside: if you wanted to kick me out of your apartment, you wouldn't have to feel bad, knowing I had a place to kick up my feet."

Kick him out? That idea sucked the air of me. "You going to drag in an air mattress?" I didn't want him to move; guess my condo wasn't as special as I thought. Not if the office was an acceptable alternative. My dad never even snoozed here, as evidenced by the lack of a couch. There was one on the first floor, but it needed to be hauled away.

Grey finished his walk around the space in front of two unmarked doors and opened each one, checking out the bathroom and storage closet.

I owed it to him to help him put his life back together, whether I liked his idea or not. I needed to suck it up and do what I could to be helpful. "You do know that I'd be your landlord?" I winked at him, which made him laugh again, and I was enjoying it. "This floor is by the far the best. I do agree with you that an empty building invites trouble. I'd thought about getting it cleaned top to bottom and fumigated, but I hadn't come up with a step two yet. I'm not sure what my dad will think when he gets back and finds that I've rented out the floors." His in particular.

"Here's what I propose: when your dad comes back, I'll move out. All of his valuables and any important papers can be stored in the safe. In the meantime, if you need room to spread your paperwork out, that oak desk is big enough for us to share."

I crossed to the window, looked down, and was surprised to see a car blow by. It was a quiet, out-of-the-way street that only attracted traffic from neighboring businesses due to being one-way with no on-ramp to the freeway.

Grey joined me. "I'm feeling adrift with all

that's happened and want to focus on what kind of a life to build going forward, not how screwed up everything is at the moment. I've started over before; this time should be a piece of cake—there's a spark that wasn't there before." His tone expressed disgust, melancholy, and a note of hope at the end.

I wanted to offer up a witty piece of advice that would garner another laugh but didn't have it and instead squeezed his hand. One of my phones dinged, breaking the silence. I pulled it out of my pocket, glanced at the screen, and read the message. "The man who ordered the hit just texted: 'paid in full.'" I scrolled down the screen for an alert from the bank and there were none. I accessed the account to verify that, and sure enough, there hadn't been a deposit. "He reneged on the final million." I called the number back. "Disconnected."

"Confident fellow. Must be certain that he can't be tracked. It's a dangerous business to hire a killer and then default. If he were dealing with a professional killer, he'd need to keep one eye open at all times." Grey hooked his arm around me. "I'm amazed someone was willing to pay a million to have me offed."

"So... he cheated me. That should make him happy. As far as I know, neither of us knows the identity of the other."

Grey locked up the office. "Let's hit up the storage unit so I can grab some clothes. Then I'll take you out to dinner." We walked down the stairs.

I locked up the building and got in the SUV, watching while Grey walked around the building and gave close scrutiny to the exterior. He then checked out the neighboring building on one side; not much to see at the city maintenance lot on the other.

"You've got two sets of glass entry doors," he said, sliding behind the wheel. "I'm thinking getting security doors installed over them should be the first step. Not the most attractive, but it will deter criminals, who'll move on to an easier mark."

"I like that idea."

Chapter Seven

The storage place was only a few miles from the office, and we made the drive in silence, each lost in thought. The unit had a combo lock, and I'd texted the code to Grey earlier, along with the address. He opened the door, and to my surprise, it looked like his possessions had been packed by professionals—everything boxed, neatly organized, and clearly marked. Grey loaded a couple of boxes into the back of the SUV.

He wanted to take me somewhere nice for dinner, which required a change of clothes, but I wasn't interested. At least not tonight. We went back to the condo, ordered in, and once again fell asleep on the couch.

I woke early for my usual Saturday morning breakfast with Rella and Avery and texted Avery that I needed a ride, thinking it was rude to leave Grey stranded. I'd finished my coffee and was attempting to scoot off the couch when he grabbed my wrist.

"It's early," he said groggily.

"My friends and I have breakfast together every Saturday."

"Hmm..." He had that cop expression, as

though attempting to ferret out more information without having to ask.

"To reassure you that you're not stuck here all day, I left a set of keys on the entry table, along with a security card."

"Breakfast takes all day?"

"We get together to catch up, dish a little gossip, and we can talk the day away." Now I sounded like I had something to hide, and I didn't. "I'm off to shower." I could feel his eyes on me as I left the room.

After showering, I sorted through my closet, choosing a bright green, paneled, sleeveless midi dress. It was perfect for what would be a sultry day, and I'd fit in with the rest of the Miami Beach crowd. Not having the patience to deal with my hair, I chose the quickest solution, scooping it off my neck and twisting it into a messy bun. I met Grey in the kitchen, and he handed me a mug of coffee. I nodded my thanks and slid onto a stool. He checked me out from head to toe and appeared irked.

"I thought you'd want to know that I sent a text to my deadbeat client: 'Pay up or watch your back,'" I told him.

"Be interesting to see if he answers. But I don't want you to do anything that puts you in danger. You might want to think about sleeping dogs… and all."

I caught myself mid-eyeroll. "While you were snoring away —"

"Which I don't do," he said with a half-smile.

"Anyway... I've got someone watching the account the client sent the money from. If the they're at all smart, they'll close it down."

"Repeating myself — you need to let it go."

"It would be helpful if we knew the identity of this person so you could make a decision as to what to do. If it's revealed that you're alive before that, then what? Move to Iceland?" He didn't appear convinced. I went on. "Another mistake: the man made the last call from a phone he hadn't used before. I was able to have it traced back to your old stomping ground — Orlando." I took my phone out of my pocket and sent a text; Grey's phone dinged. "That's from me. I started a list of suspects, and since I don't know all the players, I thought you could add to it."

"I can take it from here." To quell the outburst that was sitting on the tip of my tongue, he added, "I don't want you getting hurt."

"Got it." Barely containing my annoyance and refraining from saluting, I crossed to the sink and rinsed my mug.

Grey came up behind me, leaned in, and whispered in my ear, "You look great."

I turned, my back against the counter. "You behave yourself."

"That's rich." Grey laughed. "If I gave you the same advice?"

"For today, I can swear." I crossed my heart and squeezed past him, grabbed my purse and, with a short wave, scooted out the door.

Avery was waiting at the elevator, holding the door open. Like me, she had on a dress: a blue multi-print sleeveless tent dress. She'd opted for dark glasses that covered her face, her dark hair pulled back in a ponytail.

"How's lover boy?" she asked as the doors opened in the garage.

"He mentioned yesterday that if I wanted him to move out, he could stay at my dad's office until he figured out his next move. I'm not sure if he thinks it's what I want or it's really what he wants," I said, as we walked over and got in her Porsche.

"And you said..." She roared out onto the street.

"I nodded as though whatever he wanted would be swell. This situation is so weird. I don't know what to say and still come off as normal-ish."

"My expert opinion on men..." We both laughed, having shared dating horror stories. "Grey's probably offering you an easy out. I've seen the way he looks at you. If he does skate, he won't go far, and I can help you 'nap him again. We won't tell Rella. She can't take two kidnappings. Mum's the word." Avery crossed her lips with her finger.

"You're the best."

"Yes, I am." She tugged on a loose strand of her hair.

It was a short drive to the Cat House Café on trendy Washington Boulevard. The restaurant was owned by a friend of Rella's. She was their chief backer, her foundation supporting more than one animal rescue, along with several other charities. She always arrived ahead of us, making sure to be there when they opened. She and the owner shared a cup of coffee and used the time to discuss business.

Avery parked, and the two of us walked up to the entrance to the café and maneuvered around the line of people coming out the door, the noisy hum of dozens of conversations going on at once. The hostess waved us past, and we spotted Rella sitting at our usual window table on the outdoor patio.

While enjoying one of their amazing breakfasts or lunches, one could fall in love with and adopt one of the cats from the glassed-in room attached to the patio that had been turned into a playhouse for cats and kittens in need of a home. The occasional dog snuck in after demonstrating some get-along skills with felines. The room was dotted with oversized chairs filled with prospective parents.

Rella wore a pair of tailored ankle pants and a silk blouse; she never left the house without being perfectly groomed, not restricting her CEO look to weekdays. Besides, she was always looking for any excuse to drop by her office on her day off: "I just need to check on..." Her hundred-and-fifty-pound guard dog, Bruno, a Saint Bernard, lay asleep on her designer heels.

"How's it going today?" I asked Rella, who smiled as Avery and I sat down, the three of us facing the play area.

The server showed and set down our coffee preferences. We were well known there and made it easy by always ordering the same thing.

"The cats have been in rare form. Instead of snoozing through all the attention, they're on their game—playing and doing acrobatic leaps from one scratching post to another—and all their playfulness has increased the adoption applications." Rella beamed.

"The write-up you arranged in Miami Today will keep this place packed," I said, referring to a magazine that catered to the rich and happening.

"Your idea of featuring cat pictures in the article was a good one. I know I spent time checking each one out. I bet the ones featured get forever homes quickly." Avery smiled at Rella. "The article was so glowing that locals will flock here for the food, and be eager to brag that they adopted a pet."

"How's your victim doing?" Rella asked with a big smirk.

"Grey's resilient, that's for sure. He's moving forward, and I hope he lets me help." I finished my coffee and was tempted to wave the cup in the air for a refill.

"You know I'm the cautious one," Rella

reminded me. "Just don't let yourself get hurt or taken advantage of."

"I can't wait to dispense good advice to you." I wanted to hug her but couldn't stretch past Bruno.

"I'm the slow bloomer, not having released my inner wild child, and then there's my image, which I work hard not to tarnish. The fallout would be huge if I were to do something outrageous." Rella grimaced.

Avery and I laughed.

"I don't recommend anything illegal," I said. "I'm here to tell you that it's not that fun and definitely nerve-wracking. Would I do things differently? Maybe."

Avery's eyes went wide as she stared over my shoulder.

Rella turned her head, following Avery's surprised look. "You invited your victim?" Her brows went up.

"Would you stop? What are you talking about?" I twisted in my chair and tracked Grey's movements as he cut through the waiting patrons and bore down on the table.

"Good morning, ladies. Imagine running into you three." Grey's eyes twinkled with amusement.

I was going to have to rethink my idea that he could stay under the radar in baseball hat and sunglasses; he attracted plenty of attention—all female, young and old. He dragged a chair over from another table and sat down.

"Coincidence?" I said, an eyeroll in my tone. "I can't imagine a cat house would be your first choice of a place for breakfast."

Avery laughed. "You're forgetting that it's the newest, hottest in-spot."

Bruno lifted his head and sniffed Grey's shoe. "Nice bear you've got there." Grey patted his head.

"You're lucky Bruno didn't bite you," Rella said.

None of us except Grey looked worried. There was no chance of that happening since Bruno was a lover.

"Mobster bit off a chunk of his big toe and left holes in his back," I said with a grin.

"Exaggeration," Grey mumbled.

"Watch yourself," Rella said. "I never thought we'd find that hellion a home, but one look at Harper and he made up his mind that she was the one. He's not going to take to you poaching his territory."

"Thanks for the warning," Grey said.

"Just thinking…" Avery squinted at Grey. "You have your phone on you?" she asked me, holding out her hand.

It surprised me that she didn't have hers, but I handed mine over.

Avery flicked through the screen. "Didn't you notice there's a new tracking app on your phone?"

"So Avery is your tech guru? I wondered." Grey's eyes bored her into her, and he appeared annoyed he hadn't confirmed it before now.

"Avery's our financial advisor." I flicked my finger between Rella and myself. "She happens to be a genius with numbers. I can't recommend her highly enough." I was certain that he'd noticed I hadn't answered his question and I'd hear about it later. "Back to you, hotshot... You put a tracker on me?"

"If you weren't such a shifty chick... which I mean in the nicest way. Once I made it my mission to keep at least one eye on you, I knew I needed help, hence the app."

"You make sure that I get the exact same app for you, buddy."

The owner of the café, Prissy Mayes, came over to our table. Today's look was a white three-quarter-length spaghetti-strap dress with a flowery background, a gardenia headband holding back her long, bright-red hair, and earrings dangling to her shoulders. She held out her dagger-like nails to Grey. "You taken?"

Grey tugged to get his hand back, Prissy laughing and enjoying every moment. He draped his arm across the back of my chair.

"Lucky you," Prissy said to me and shot Grey a pout. "Your regulars?" she asked the rest of us.

"Do you like waffles?" I asked Grey, and he nodded. I looked at Prissy. "Double my order." I turned back to Grey. "You're going to love the food."

"The donations have tripled today." Prissy shot Rella a thumbs up and gave her a quick hug as she got called away.

"I have a bit of news," Avery said. "The building where I have my office was sold. The new owner came around, and to say we didn't hit it off would be an understatement. I didn't mean to call him a dick face, it just slipped out. After that, he repeated that he wouldn't be holding me to my lease and that I could move out twice in a two-minute conversation. Pronto was implied but not said. He claimed it was a one-time, take-it-or-leave-it offer. I gave notice on the spot."

"I can make a couple of calls and find you something by tomorrow," Rella offered. "Same area?"

"I have a place in mind, if Harper goes for it." Avery turned a sneaky smile on me. "I'd like to rent one of the floors in your father's building. I drove by and love it."

"You're in luck. I rented the third floor just yesterday." I shot a sideways glance at Grey. "You can have your choice of the first or second floors. Even though you did a drive-by, I feel compelled to remind you that it's a mediocre location at best—under the freeway, almost anyway. The upside is the building is insulated from traffic noise."

"Don't you think you need something more upscale?" Rélla wrinkled her nose. "I'm certain I can find you something on Ocean. That way, your clients won't have to worry about getting out of their cars."

"It's not that bad," Grey defended.

Thankfully, the stuffed waffles arrived at the table just then, putting an end to that conversation. Each plate was piled with waffles three high, eggs, cheese, bacon and peppers between the layers. A ring of strawberries decorated the outside of the plate, along with a dash of whipped cream.

"How do you eat this?" Grey asked.

"You topple it and dig in." Avery demonstrated with her fork.

Grey didn't join in the conversation. Except for the occasional comment, he focused his attention on the restaurant and checking out the neighboring tables. In between bites, he assessed each of us and watched how we interacted.

I wanted to ask about whatever conclusions he came to, but another time.

Eventually, Grey leaned back in his chair. "That was amazingly good. I can see why there's a line to get in."

A server came by and refilled our coffees.

"What are your plans?" Rella asked Grey.

"It's only been a few days," I reminded her.

"I'm staying in Miami. Easier for Harper to keep an eye on me. She saved my life, so she's responsible for it. Isn't that how it works?" He smirked at me.

"This means I tell you what to do and you do it." I smirked back.

He stared at my lips until my cheeks heated up. "We'll see how that works out for you."

"You have a brother?" Avery asked.

"Ditch the ugly frames, and you'll have the men lined up," Grey said. She'd pushed her sunglasses up on her head, and her topaz eyes sparkled. "If you need someone to pre-screen them, I'm your man. I can spot a loser and kick his ass to the curb before he takes up your time."

Prissy came back and stared at Grey's clean plate. "How was it?"

"I was tempted to lick the plate." Grey rubbed his stomach. "You happen to have a wagon, so I can get a ride to the car?"

Prissy laughed. "Love the compliments, charmer."

Chapter Eight

We said our good-byes and went our separate ways. I rode with Grey, and we'd barely pulled away from the restaurant when my phone rang. I took it out of my pocket and smiled at the screen. "You staying out of trouble?" I asked upon answering.

"What would be the fun in that?" Gram unleashed a growly laugh. "You wouldn't give me your shifty friend's number before, and I need it now."

"Gram... why do you need it?" I asked in a demanding, no-nonsense tone that she couldn't miss, since it was reminiscent of her own.

It was Ender's contact info that Gram wanted, and a good thing she didn't know the man she wanted to speak to was her neighbor's grandson. No one knew he was a behind-the-scenes fixer, and he wanted it to stay that way. I knew because we'd grown up together, but I'd been sworn to secrecy years back. When he got in trouble, I covered for him.

"It's not for me. It's for my neighbor's granddaughter," Gram huffed. "I'm only calling because this friend of yours has fixed problems in the past. If this guy is as badass as you've intimated, then why don't you have his number? I think you do and you're holding out. You need to be reminded that I didn't get this old without knowing how to take care of myself."

"Listen up, sweetcakes, I'm about to hit you with your own words. Somewhere along the line, you've misplaced your common sense, which I'm sure told you to stay out of other people's business."

Grey laughed.

I knocked his arm and put my finger across my lips.

"That's rich coming from you," Gram said in exasperation. "I don't know what your excuse is, but it's not old age."

I glanced at the clock on the dash. "I can be there in an hour, and we can have a long talk."

"Just give me the damn name," Gram snapped.

"I'm bringing pie. Do you need anything else?"

"Wahoo. Now you're talking. You may be annoying, but you know the way to my heart."

We hung up, and I tossed the phone in the cup holder. "I'm going to need the car for several hours. You can drop yourself off."

"Nice try, sweetheart. I'll drive. I feel compelled to get you to wherever you're going in one piece." Grey's tone held amusement, and his eyes bored into me, daring me to argue. "Can't wait to meet Gram. We stopping at the grocery store for that pie?"

I made a barfing noise.

"Gotcha, that would be a no. Program that thing so I know where I'm going." He waved at the GPS.

I had the address for Patisserie Bakery on my phone and programmed it in, then called and reserved a key lime pie. "I'm issuing the strongest of warnings." I shifted in my seat. "When I'm done, you're going to want to catch an Uber back to the condo."

"And miss out on pie? It better be good." Grey cruised through the streets, sticking to the speed limit, which was more than I could say for myself when I was behind the wheel.

"Gram is an outspoken woman. Whatever she has on her mind, she'll share. Trust me, when she meets you, she's going to shoot a hundred questions at you and want to know your intentions. When she gets a head of steam going, they'll get more personal. I'll do my best to keep her under control, but my success rate is low. Beware: if you pass muster, she'll start plotting to call in a preacher."

Grey laughed. "I've got experience with hardened criminals. I can handle one older lady."

I turned and looked out the window.

"If you're going to roll your eyes, do it to my face."

I bit my lip to keep from laughing. "The

bakery's up here. Parking is sparse, so you can drop me off and I'll run in. I wouldn't recommend coasting in the red zone; they ticket around here."

Grey mumbled to himself, which amused me.

As we got closer, I jabbed my finger at the windshield.

He coasted to a stop in front of the bakery, and I hopped out and raced inside. There was no wait, and I was back out in a couple of minutes. Grey timed it just right, pulling back up as I stepped off the curb.

I got in and reset the GPS. "Another heads up: Morningside at the Beach caters to partying eccentrics. They're a rowdy bunch and like their fun. They have every amenity available and, thus far, have kept the craziness on the property."

Grey got on the Interstate and exited north of Ft. Lauderdale, heading towards the water. The retirement community was on the A1A across from the beach. He turned in, and the guard, catching sight of my sticker, raised the arm and waved us in.

"Follow this road until you see a cherry red '57 Thunderbird sitting in a driveway."

"An old rust bucket that no one wants to steal? Even then, I'd think it would be gone in a half-second, if only for the parts."

I chuckled to myself. "Park in the driveway."

"Someone you know?" Grey slowed for a woman in the middle of the road who was waving wildly.

Gram had dressed for the occasion—a tropical print tent dress on her skinny frame and a hat with a parrot on top, which had me doing a double take.

Grey pulled into the driveway, and I got out. "Don't say I didn't warn you." I left him to ogle the pristine rust bucket.

Gram rushed over and wrapped her arms me, giving me a hard hug and covering my cheek in kisses. "My little girl been behaving herself?"

"You of all people know there's no fun in that."

Grey grabbed the pie box and smiled at the woman checking him out.

"Who's this looker?" Gram gushed, her big brown eyes running leisurely over him.

I elbowed Gram with a *stop it* look on my face. "A new friend." I winked at Grey.

"Hey, son-of-a-gun." The words came out of the beak of the parrot sitting on her hat.

On closer inspection, I determined that the colorful parrot was stuffed and somehow affixed to the top of the hat. I sighed with relief, having originally worried it was real.

Gram held out a small remote. "Isn't Bogo the cutest? I had it specially made. I have to be careful letting him talk outside, as he's not always appropriate. I should've thought of that before choosing the phrases."

I shook my head. "Grey Walker, this is my

Gram, Jean Winters."

He bent over her outstretched hand, kissing the back, and I thought she'd swoon.

"You can call me Gram," she said in a giggly tone.

"We need to get this in the refrigerator before it melts in the sweltering heat." I pointed to the box Grey was holding.

Gram rushed to open the door into the living space—a two-bedroom unit with its own patio, the living and dining rooms together with a kitchen on one side. I'd helped her decorate, and we'd had fun choosing comfortable furniture.

I took the box and handed it to Gram, who rushed it into the kitchen and came back licking her fingers. "So good," she moaned.

"You spit on it so you wouldn't have to share, didn't you?" I admonished, winking at her.

"When you get to be my age, you can't wait to be doing stuff, and that includes that delicious pie, which tastes like sin." Gram pointed to a couple of oversized chairs, then took a pad and pen off a nearby credenza and handed it to me. "Write down the information for that Shark character. Don't tell me you don't remember, cuz you and I know that you don't forget squat." She trotted back to the kitchen.

I put the pad on a side table. "Hope you like iced tea," I said to Grey.

"I like your Gram."

"If you were a bit older, she'd hop you."

"So we're clear, I'm taken." Grey winked.

"I wouldn't phrase it that way. Remember that preacher I mentioned? I forgot to tell you he lives down the road and can be here before you blink."

Grey shook his head, a grin on his face. "You better not let it slip that you've already compromised me."

Gram came out, tray in hand with glasses lined up on it, along with a pitcher of iced tea and a bowl of Pop Tart bites. She set it on the coffee table.

There was a thundering banging on the door. Grey jumped to his feet. "Do you want me to get it?"

Gram gave him a moony smile and hooked her arm in his. "Let's go together." She patted his biceps.

Grey opened the door.

Ender Perry inched into the entry and came to a halt. "What are you doing here?" he demanded.

Gram made the introductions.

"Don't want to interrupt anything," Ender boomed. "I saw Trouble's car parked out front and thought I'd say hello." He maneuvered his considerable bulk into the living room with a certain amount of grace. "How's it going?" He waved, a patented smirk on his lips that he never went anywhere without.

I waved back. I hadn't move out of my chair

since I was able to hear everything that was said.
Ender wanted something. It would be interesting
to see how he contrived to get me away for a
chat. "Gram, I looked through my phone and
don't have contact info for Shark." I turned to
Ender. "You wouldn't happen to have a number
for him, would you?" Gram didn't notice my
sarcasm, but Grey did, his eyes boring into the
two of us.

No one at the retirement village knew that
Ender Perry, aka Shark, had another life, one that
was shady as heck, and that included his
grandmother. The moniker had been bestowed
on him when he went into business as a private
money lender, and he still used it when he didn't
want his name associated with whatever deal he
had going.

Ender noted Grey's intense stare and returned
it in spades. "Interesting that we're all old
friends." He twirled his finger. "Growing up
together. Grey and I went to the same elementary
school, and Harper and I met when she moved in
with her Gram. Being older and more
responsible, I did my best to be a good
influence."

I choked back a snort.

"Harper was always game to tag along,
whether invited or not... You know how trouble
is—it finds some people because they're up to the
challenge." Ender winked at me, both of us
knowing he was full of it. "Then, good friend

that I was, I'd step up to bail her out with a believable story for her Gram."

Gram snorted frighteningly loud. "Some of those stories were horse-doo, but you were such a sweet boy and always my favorite on the block."

"That's because Ender would sneak you cigarettes, sit on the back porch, and trade outrageous stories with you," I said.

"How would you know that, young lady?"

"You really are getting old, Gram." I almost laughed at her look of outrage. "There was a window right above the stoop, and I oiled the hinges so I could hang my head out without being heard. It paid to know what the two of you were BSing each other about. Ignore Ender's innocent look—the best one he can muster anyway—he knew I was up there. He'd raise his head and grin when you turned to blow smoke into the neighbor's yard."

"That would've been cool—blowing smoke in any direction I pleased." Gram mimicked inhaling and whooshing out.

"Gram and I went cold turkey together." Ender patted her gnarled hand. "Though I suspect she's cheated a time or two."

Gram blushed.

Grey, who'd been silently assessing Ender as though trying to make a connection, spoke up. "I remember you now. You were always getting kicked out of school for thuggish behavior.

Mostly kicking butt. Thankfully, mine was never on your list."

"I was totally misunderstood as a kid," Ender said with a smarmy smile. "Most times, I got the finger of blame when I hadn't done a thing."

Grey laughed, the *good one* left unsaid.

"You know, Gram, since Ender's here, maybe he can help you with your problem." I almost laughed at Gram trying to act like she didn't know what I was talking about. "You know the problem—the one that wouldn't be one if you minded your own business."

"Harper Finn." Gram shot me a 'behave' squint-eye.

Oops! Full name. I knew her well enough to know that she wasn't so much mad as exasperated.

Grey raised his hand. "Maybe I can help."

"You're such a sweet boy."

I looked down and laughed.

Ender grunted. "Tell me what you need."

"It doesn't kill a person to be helpful if they can," Gram said.

The three of us stared expectantly.

"You know April? Pam Manning's lovely granddaughter?"

"The hot young blonde that trots around here in a skimpy bikini, giving an eyeful to the old men rocking on their porches?" I said.

"If this is about the ex-boyfriend not taking no for an answer, I'll tell you the same thing I told

my granny: Butt out. It's being taken care of."
Ender stared Gram down, which didn't
intimidate her in the least; in fact, she smiled at
the man.

"Now promise me that you won't pitch the
bastard's body in the lake." Gram nodded
toward the sliding door. "Sooner or later, it'll
float to the top. Then eww."

Ender unleashed an aggrieved sigh. "I'm not a
killer," he said emphatically, as though we
needed to be reminded. "I'm certain such drastic
measures won't be called for. Brady's been
warned that I better not ever hear another word
about his scrawny ass."

"Or what?" I asked, trying to tame the smirk.
Ender ignored me.

"You were my first choice. I even had my
phone in hand." Gram smiled at Ender. "But I
was with your *grandmother* at the time – you
know she detests you calling her Granny – and
she reminded me, not that I needed it, that you're
a successful businessman and your attention is
needed elsewhere. I called Harper, who wasn't
the least bit helpful."

"I brought pie." I wondered if Gram knew the
extent of Ender's business enterprises.

Gram's house phone rang, and she jumped up
and trotted back to the kitchen.

"Is Brady still alive?" I asked once she was out
of earshot.

"Of course he is." Ender shook his head and

turned to Grey. "Sorry to hear about your arrest; you were always a tight-ass, goody-two-shoes type, and I want you to know I never believed that you did it. And if you had, you wouldn't have been dumb enough to dump the body on your property."

Grey's mouth tightened.

I cut in and asked, "What are you doing here?"

"I came to tell Gram to keep her nose out of April's situation. I knew something was up and had to strong-arm my granny for the details. Before you jump to the wrong conclusion…" He eyed me. "I threatened to cancel our weekly dinner. Once I got the details, I knew without having to ask that my granny had offered to help get up in the not-so-lovebirds' business. We both know full well that expecting our grannies to mind their own business, even after requesting help, would be wishful thinking."

If Gram heard him use "granny" to describe her, she'd relocate that big head of his.

Ender hefted his bulk out of the chair and scanned the room, then focused on the kitchen. "I thought we'd have a few words outside."

"You want to talk to Harper, I'll be right by her side," Grey said. "So why don't you sit back down and tell us what's on your mind?"

"Nothing to do with you, dude. I halfway like you, old time's sake and all." Ender leveled a shifty smile at him. "I'd like nothing more than to sit here in the cool air, except Gram hung up several minutes ago and has been eavesdropping ever since."

"Am not," Gram yelled as she marched back into the room, not the least bit embarrassed that she'd been caught. "I have to run next door, so you can sit right here." She thoroughly scrutinized the three of us but didn't say anything more and, without another word, banged out the front door.

"So you two are a…" Ender waved his pudgy finger around, sitting back down. "You need to stop thinking with your…" He pointed at Grey's crotch. "I'll remind you again, Mr. Straight and Narrow — also humorless, as I recall — this one is trouble and wouldn't make a good match for you." He was back to waving his finger around.

Trouble? He had some nerve. "My foray into… whatever I was doing… is over," I told him in an irritated tone. "For your information, and so you won't worry your pretty head, I closed up shop and dumped the burners." Maybe I saved one or two. None of Ender's business. "Even though you suggested it, I decided to take credit if anyone asks. I'm now renting out the office building and focusing on Finn Media." Among other things that were none of his business.

"Sounds good." Ender snorted. "Until you turn around and stick your nose into someone else's business. It runs in the family, and you won't be able to help yourself. So next time you call, I'll remind you of your high and mightiness and hang up."

"No need to worry about Harper," Grey told Ender in an even tone. "She's got backup anytime she needs it."

"You've got it bad." Ender shook his head and turned to me. "Keep an eye on your Gram—yours and mine, as they're already up to something else. I can smell it. I caught them whispering together earlier and called them out. Both straight out lied to my face."

I laughed, which earned me a hair-raising glare. Would've loved to have a ringside seat when that went down.

Annoyed with me, Ender turned his attention to Grey. "It would be a good idea to swap out your car. I can get one delivered tomorrow."

"Let me guess, you're my nephew?"

Ender grinned. "Harper was in over her head and confided the predicament she'd got herself into answering a phone that wasn't hers. When I heard the details, I suggested she throw the phone in the Atlantic and move on. We know how that worked out—in one ear and out the other. She laid out her so-called plan. I did my best to unravel the runaround without choking her to death. I thought she was ballsy, but those that know her know she's got a pair. From the start, she did her best to be light on details. Had I known you were the ex-cop, I still would've advised her to mind her own business, but I'd have tipped you off." Ender shot me a toothy grin, then looked back at Grey. "You've been given fair warning—are you up to the challenge that is Harper Finn?"

I glared at Ender. "You're going to have to derail our grandmothers from discovering Shark's identity. Unless you're ready for that grilling." I knew the questions would be never-ending, and so did he.

"Shark is dead. Only a handful of people know me by that name, and none have the cajones to call me that now that I've issued the stop order." Ender swiveled his neck around, checking out the room suspiciously, as though Gram had managed to sneak back in without us noticing. "Those two old broads are sneaky as hell, but they're outmatched." He heaved himself to his feet and strode around the room, stopping in front of the buffet, his beady-eyed gaze zeroing in on something. He picked it up—it looked like a handheld radio or walkie-talkie—turned it in his hands, then dropped it on the floor and crushed it under his foot. "We were being recorded. I'm going to wring Granny's neck. Neither of those old broads can claim immunity; they're thick as thieves."

"Were they listening this whole time?" I eyed the mangled mess. "Gram's going to demand payment."

"I guess we'll find out," Ender growled. "It's

always something around here. Usually no big deal. In order to protect them from the fallout from their do-gooder activities, they need a go-to man they can rely on, and I don't have the time." Ender shifted his attention to Grey. "You were a PI—technically still are. Looking for some legit job referrals? The jobs would consist of grandkids in their twenties and thirties sucking off Daddy's dime, their rich parents willing to pay to get them out of trouble." He reached in his pocket, handing Grey a business card. "Call me if you're interested."

The front door opened, and Gram popped her head inside. "All clear?"

Ender stood. "I better not hear you're in trouble, because that would mean that my granny is knee-deep along with you. That would put you both on my s-list."

Gram grinned. That was like waving a red flag at her, but he knew her well enough to know that and didn't need me reminding him.

Ender nodded in my direction and said to Grey, "If you're going to... you know... remember you need to keep a tight rein." He paused on his way to the door, picked up the mangled plastic, and handed it to Gram. "No bueno."

"You big lug." Gram growled.

Chapter Nine

It was bingo night at the rec center, and Gram insisted we tag along. Grey shook his head furiously at me over her shoulder, so I begged off, claiming dinner plans, and we left. We dined at a burger drive-thru and went back to the condo. He had a hundred questions, which I was able to put off because my phone rang—a client's file needed attention and now. I knew it would come up again, though.

I woke every morning at the crack of dawn and set up my workspace on the balcony or, when weather wouldn't permit, the kitchen island, holding virtual meetings with my staff not far from the coffee pot. Thankfully, everyone on staff came with a high degree of organization. It made it easy to keep the clients happy.

I heard Grey's footsteps come up behind me, and he bent down and kissed my cheek. "Coffee's ready." I pointed to the pot I'd made, having already drunk two cups. I'd finished with everything that needed immediate attention. Clicking over to my email, I found a new one from Avery on Grey's past acquaintances.

Grey grabbed a mug and claimed the stool across from me, setting his phone down. "You always awake this early?"

I nodded. "Love mornings. If I jump on everything that needs my attention first thing, I can get a lot done."

"I've been busy myself. I've got a crew coming to the office building to clean it from top to bottom and haul the trash out of the first floor."

"Let me guess—you called your buddy Ender?" I asked.

"I was tempted to rib the man about his alter ego but decided it was juvenile. Instead, I got straight to the point and told him what I needed. He was more than happy to help."

"His annoying habit of cracking his knuckles is enough to keep people in line." I laughed. "Although I notice he hasn't been doing it as much lately. His given name and burly physique are enough to put the scare into most people."

"I've been thinking over his offer of client referrals. He confided without much prodding that he's left anything illegal in his past; that happened years ago, and he now specializes in loaning money to real estate investors. Something goes south, and the property guarantees the loan. I did tell him that I'd never turn a blind eye to murder."

I groaned.

"No worries. He laughed it off. I'll admit it was an unsettling sound. Considering the duplicitous life I'm leading, I dialed back the moral high ground."

"You're really not. I did a little research, and it's not a crime to not come forward and say, 'Hey I'm alive.' Also, Ender knows your true identity and wants to work with you." I finished off the last drop of my coffee. "As for Ender, as you know, I've known him for a number of years, and his name's never been linked to a murder. A couple of broken faces, yes. The story is that they threw the first punch."

"Good to know." Grey eyed my stack of paperwork. "Are you staying out of trouble today? Keeping your clients happy?"

"I can multi-task." That wasn't the right response, considering the growl he unleashed. "I'm about to move out to the patio and go through everything again, make sure I didn't miss anything. I hate to waste a gorgeous, sunny day."

"Why do I feel like I'm missing something?"

I did have a couple of questions for him. Now was probably better than later, and he couldn't accuse me of being evasive. Not too much anyway. "Don't you think it's odd that Mindy Graham's father isn't pushing for a murder investigation? You'd think he'd want someone brought to justice."

Grey got up and poured another cup of coffee. "Or Graham thinks the real culprit, meaning me, got away and is satisfied because I'm dead."

"Jeff Graham certainly has the dough to fund a hit, but there haven't been any large withdrawals from any of his accounts. Still checking, but so far, no off-shore accounts have shown up."

"What the hell are you up to?" Grey turned my laptop around and scanned the screen. "Where did you get this report?"

"I forwarded you a copy as you walked in." I grabbed my computer back. "I don't know if you've given any thought to assuming the Steve Smith identity." He didn't answer, so I continued. "Would you be happy being Steve and letting Grey Walker rest in peace? Or do you want to continue to be Grey and hope you don't get pulled over? When a check comes back that you're dead, then what?"

"I can call myself anything I want as long as I don't use phony ID to establish said identity, and I'm not doing that," he said adamantly. "What I don't want is you sticking your neck out and getting it snapped off."

"Ouch." I made a face.

"It's hard to believe that you went to the trouble of checking out Graham but aren't going to follow through."

"It's not like I'm planning to meet with the man in person." Not yet anyway.

Grey groaned. "Repeat after me…" He held up his right hand and nodded for me to do the same. "I solemnly swear not to go knocking on anyone's door asking questions."

I dropped my hand, which I'd only raised shoulder high. "I won't go without you." I flashed him a cheesy smile.

"Pinky swear." Grey held his out, then looped it around mine and gripped it tight.

I decided a change of subject was in order before I blurted out another of my new ideas. "The elevator at the office needs to be inspected to make sure it's safe and probably needs an operating license. I'm not certain what the rules are. I don't want Avery or her clients getting stuck inside."

"I put that on the list of things that need attention. When your dad shows up, will he be okay with all the changes? The biggest one being that once the security door is installed, he won't have a key."

"I hope to have that problem."

"You mind if I strand you here today? I'd like to go to the office for a couple of hours," Grey asked and then mumbled, "At least I'll know where you're at. I'm getting an SUV delivered later this afternoon, and I need to be here when my new ride gets dropped off. Ender hooked me up with a car dealer friend, which made the process easy. Even threw in an extended warranty." Grey grabbed my mug and his, rinsed them out, and put them in the dishwasher. He came and pulled me to my feet and into his arms. "You need anything, call."

* * *

Hours later, having moved my office outside and set everything up on the glass table, I was trying not to focus all my attention on the beach below. I'd finished everything on my to-do list and then some. This was a day when the ability to multi-task came in handy. I pulled out a pad and scribbled down questions regarding Grey's situation as they popped into my head, with a separate column for random ideas.

I'd finally had enough; my brain felt stuffed. I got up and grabbed a baseball hat and sunglasses and headed down to the white sand, taking pleasure in digging my toes in and feeling the slight breeze against my cheeks. Then I ventured into the water and ran along the shoreline, kicking my aggressions out into the bay. My phone rang, keeping me from getting totally soaked. Grey's number popped up. I needed to take a pic of him to go with his number but didn't know how long he'd keep the burner phone.

I answered, and before I could say anything, he snapped, "Where are you?"

"Where are you?"

"Just answer the question."

I gave an exaggerated salute; anyone out on the water would be impressed. "Okay. But you first."

There were a few seconds of silence, before he

said, "Your living room, looking for you."

"Walk out to the patio."

"You're not out here."

"Look over the railing." I paused and asked, "Do you see a nutjob waving wildly? That would be me." I pulled it off with one hand.

"How do I get down there?"

"Take the elevator down to the garage, and there's an exit at the back that puts you almost on the beach. I'll come meet you." I loitered in the water until I saw the door open, then hiked up the sand.

Grey pulled me into his arms and hugged me hard. "I thought you were off stirring up trouble." He clasped my hand in his, and we walked back to the shoreline. "I'm back earlier than I thought because, frankly, I was in the way at the office. Ender sent over a more competent crew than I expected. The head guy, Hugo, came prepared with his guys, and they got busy hauling out the trash. The man even thought to bring a dumpster with him."

"I'm happy to be losing my slumlord status." I looked up and grinned.

"Avery stopped by. Chatted it up with Hugo. You'd think they were old friends, rather than just meeting for the first time. She snapped dozens of pictures of her floor and wants a rental agreement."

"A handshake will have to suffice. It's not like I'm going to kick her out."

"It's Avery's idea that you rent the floors as-is, and if anyone wants changes, they can do the work themselves."

"Sounds good. I'm going to keep the top floor as storage and let the first floor stand empty until the smell dissipates."

Grey wrinkled his nose. "Hugo asked me what the heck. Disgruntled tenant? I didn't know and, using one of your tricks, let him assume what he wanted."

"Happy to be a good influence." I ignored his snort. "I hate to plead ignorance, but my dad really did keep his business dealings to himself."

"Before Avery roared off in her Carrera, she hit me with a hundred questions, letting me know after the interrogation that should I do anything to hurt you, there were a variety of wild animals around that could use a good meal."

"Now that's a good friend."

Grey laughed. "I have a confession. You left your files strewn across the table on the patio, and they taunted me to take a look, especially the notepad with my name at the top. I thought, 'What would Harper do?' Then flicked through the pages."

I could hardly put up an argument that I wouldn't do such a thing when we both knew I would. "That will teach me to clean up after myself."

"Your brainstorming about me was an interesting read, especially the notes and questions pertaining to Mindy Graham's death. Your list of suspects was short. Not sure why you think Jeff Graham would kill his own daughter."

"I don't, but he'd be interesting to talk to, get his perspective. I planned to ask you to add to the list, since I have no clue who had contact with the deceased other than family members." I peered up at him to gauge his irritation. Grey was a lot calmer than I thought he'd be. "You ready for me to pitch my new idea? It's a way for me to fill up some of the blank space on that pad."

Grey groaned.

"Keep an open mind." I dug my feet in the sand and came to a stop, then stepped in front of him so we were face to face. "I cleared my calendar for this new project I'm thinking about. What better cover is there than an author researching their next project? It would be natural for me to be asking questions and attempting to arrange interviews for my upcoming book... so I could do justice to the story of Mindy Graham's death."

"I hate to be a killjoy..."

No he didn't, but I kept a bland expression.

"You start asking questions and the murderer gets wind of it, he or she will quickly decide that you're an irritant that needs to be dealt with."

"If we're discussing the pros and cons, that's definitely a con," I said. His face tightened. "I'm only in the note-taking stage," I said, attempting to placate him. "If I decide to take it to the next step, I'll talk to you first. How's that?"

Grey bent down until we were nose to nose. "You want to know what I think? You're full of it. You uncover something, and you'll be off."

"Maybe not." I struggled not to laugh, then stepped back and kicked water on him.

Grey looked down at his wet jeans. "You picked the wrong man to drench."

"Sissy."

He charged forward, and my attempt to evade his outstretched arms was futile; he grabbed me up and walked me into the waves, dropping me into the water. I squealed and stumbled back. Grey's arm shot out. He caught me and, with a shift of momentum, took us both down into the salty seawater. He rolled to a sitting position and pulled me on top of him.

"I realize that getting you to drop this investigation is pointless." He tightened his hold as a small wave washed over us. "Give me your word that you won't be going off on a wild hair, that you'll talk to me first. In person, sitting across a table from one another. Don't think about blowing me off in some rushed phone call."

I reached out with my finger, crossing his heart and then mine. "Promise. In the spirit of being upfront, the first person I'm going to interview is you."

"I knew that was coming."

"You know you want answers. I want to help you get them. If you come up with a better idea than me impersonating a writer, I'm all ears."

Grey dumped me off his lap and scooped me up, setting me in the ankle-deep water.

I took off running.

He chased me up the beach, swinging me off my feet and tossing me over his shoulder as he walked inside.

Chapter Ten

Grey set me on my feet, grabbed my hand, and ushered me into the elevator. We rode to the top in silence.

I showered and pulled on a sleeveless turquoise t-shirt dress with a deep side slit, one of my favorite things to wear around the house, and went out to the kitchen, taking a seat at the island.

Grey was wearing a pair of sweatpants that hung low on his hips and a t-shirt stretched across his abs, a kitchen towel tucked in the front of his pants. He'd seasoned a couple of steaks and was chopping vegetables. He'd also uncorked a bottle of Cabernet, my favorite, from a California winery that I'd yet to try.

"I'll take a glass."

"Oh no you don't." He whisked the bottle off the counter and disappeared out to the balcony, coming back empty-handed. "I've got a romantic evening planned, and I need that bottle to carry it off."

I tried to remember if there was a lime in the refrigerator. When Grey put the steaks on the barbecue, I planned to sneak a shot of tequila to calm my fluttering heart.

"You've got that 'I'm up to something' look on your face. Might as well fess up now. You know I'll get it out of you." Grey's steely blue eyes bored into me.

The glint of humor had me relaxing. I slid off the stool and opened the cupboard. "Would you like a pre-dinner shot?" I pulled out a bottle of Patron.

Grey eyed me. "I don't want you getting sauced before dinner."

"One drink." I held up a finger. "Two's my max. Three, and it's 'dancing on the table' time."

"Pour me one."

I watched as he took the platter out to the balcony and stood at the barbecue with his back to me. Then I cut up a lime, filled a small glass, grabbed two shot glasses and the bottle, set everything on a tray, and followed him outside. He'd already set the table and moved it closer to the railing.

I set the tray down on a side table and filled the glasses, handing one to Grey. "You're full of surprises."

Grey took the glass from my outstretched hand, and we clinked glasses and downed them. "It's about time I showed off a few of my talents. I love to cook, and I'm good at it. Haven't had anyone get sick yet."

"Good to know about the sick part. Just to be on the safe side, I'll take a test taste before eating." I grinned at him. "My talents consist of buying prepared fresh foods that go in the oven. That, and I know where all the good restaurants are located." I sat in the nearest chair and leaned my head back, inhaling the slight scent of salt on the breeze. "If there's anything I can do…" I knew I was probably worrying for nothing, but I hoped this didn't turn out to be an evening of good news/really sucky news.

It was the start of a perfect evening. The temp had dropped, along with the humidity, and the sky was colored in shades of yellow and pink as the sun set.

Grey finished cooking dinner and served up the plates, sitting next to me and filling my wine glass. "To interesting beginnings," he toasted.

The man knew his way around the kitchen. He'd paired the seasoned steaks with grilled vegetables and potato wedges in herbs, and everything tasted as good as it smelled. Once the dishes were cleared away, we moved to a double chaise with a view out over the water.

Grey hooked his arm around me. "It was pointed out to me that I should stop being a 'horse's ass' and admit my feelings to you before you move on and leave me to moon over you."

The horse reference was a dead giveaway that Avery had unloaded what she thought were words of wisdom on the man. I wish I'd been there or that she'd sent over a recording. I bit back a laugh as I looked up at him.

"Would you go steady with me?" He raised his brows, a smile on his face.

"Since we're living together…" I covered my face and laughed. "And when someone asks, 'How did you two meet?'" I asked in a prissy tone and laughed again.

"Harper kidnapped my heart." Grey clasped a hand to his chest.

"Good thing the rest of you came along with it."

"Don't be a romance downer." Grey tightened his hold. "If anyone does ask, we go with the truth—we met over coffee. I've been told that I've got a 'none of your business attitude,' so it's unlikely that anyone would ask."

"I'm hoping that going steady means you're staying." I snuggled closer to his side.

"The only thing that would have me rethinking this living arrangement is if I brought trouble to your door."

"Even if you were to cross paths with someone from your previous life, I doubt they'd recognize you." I ran my finger across his short beard. "Another thing you've got going for you—no one is looking for you. And even if someone *did* follow you here, no one's getting up to the top floor. We have the best security."

Grey turned my face to his and kissed me.

Chapter Eleven

Another beautiful morning, and I'd commandeered the patio table again. I'd finished up video chats with employees and just sent my last email until they filled up my inbox again. I glanced up and watched as Grey approached. "You going to the office?" My stomach growled, reminding me that coffee wasn't a meal.

Grey wrinkled his nose. "Hugo found evidence of rats and is fumigating the place."

"That's disgusting."

"Ender referred a client to me. Thought you might like to ride along and witness the master at work."

"I'm honored that you would ask... unless you have an ulterior motive." I eyed him suspiciously.

"It's easier to keep an eye on you if you're in the passenger seat."

"How are you going to introduce me? Probably better not to say we're cohabitating. Or doing it. Partner would be better." I gave him a cheeky smile.

"As long as we're agreed that as senior

member of this team, I'm the lead and you'll follow my direction. Any disagreements are to be had out of earshot of the client."

"Yes, sir." I jumped up and curtsied, then scrutinized him in his blue jeans and button-down. "I'll change." I'd figure out something that wasn't pants, since they cut off your circulation in nine-hundred-degree heat. I settled on a cotton skirt and sleeveless top and slid into a pair of slip-on sandals, then grabbed a briefcase purse and met Grey in the living room.

Grey whistled. He grabbed my hand, and we went out to the elevator and down to the garage. This was the first that I was seeing his new black Escalade; it had been detailed, and the exterior shone. I checked out the tag in the window, and everything appeared to be legal-like. He'd told me that the swap had gone off with a hitch.

He held open the door, and I got in and checked out the immaculate interior. When he got behind the wheel, I said, "Nice ride."

"I thought about going with another color but figured I'd fit in with the hundreds of other black SUVs on the road. The dealer joked that it was the hottest-selling color." Grey pulled out of the garage and onto the street.

"You know where you're going?"

"I thought you'd program the GPS." He pointed to the unit and handed me his phone.

It wasn't hard to find the message with the address, since there was only one. "I know where this is. I can tell you where to go."

Grey laughed. "The romance is dead already."

"On second thought, you're not going to like me jabbing my finger this way and that." I went ahead and programmed in the address. "Tell me about this job."

"The client, Simon Kent, owns a string of strip joints and other businesses, from which he's recently discovered that his son, Wilson, has been siphoning off money." Grey turned onto the Causeway.

"Call the cops, case solved."

"Do you want to hear the rest or be surprised?"

"I'm not fond of half-assed stories, so go ahead, my dear." I readjusted the seat and settled back to listen, figuring I couldn't fool with all the buttons at the same time.

"Little bast— figured out his father was onto him, disappeared in the middle of the night, and is lying low. I suggested that Wilson's probably skipped town, but Kent claims the kid doesn't have the smarts."

"How old is this larcenous fellow? You find him, then what?"

"Kent wants to hire me to track down Junior, who's pushing fifty, and persuade him to return the money. It's not good for the rich to have bad publicity about wayward family members." There was an eyeroll in his tone, which made me smile. "The business is structured as a corporation, and Kent has stockholders to answer to. They're not going to be happy and will hold him accountable."

I snorted. "Hate to break it to the old man, but I'm betting that there's very little money left, if any. I doubt Wilson used it to fund a retirement plan."

"Pretty much what I said." Grey caught my smirk and added, "Close anyway. This is a meet-and-greet to see if I pass Kent's high standards."

"Whatever." I sniffed. "If he's going to put you through the dick-around dance, you need to double your hourly rate."

"Kent told me upfront that he wasn't going to be hosed; he knew the going rate. Just because his attitude irritated me, I raised my fee and he didn't argue, which told me he was blustering and full of himself."

"What's your plan, hotshot?"

Grey gave me an amused look. "Told Kent to make a list of the son's friends, and that includes any girlfriends, since there's no wife. I got a referral to a hacker and am hoping that tapping Wilson's phone will make him easy to find."

"If your hacker is the least bit dicey, I've got someone who can get the job done."

"Of course you do." Grey shook his head. "What are you mumbling?"

"Just wondering how you're going to introduce yourself, what name you're going to use. Since we're partners, I should at least get your name right. Then there's the issue of my name."

"It'll be a surprise." He winked.

"Bad idea," I mumbled.

"I can hear you."

It was a short drive up the Causeway to Palm Island. He exited and took the road over the bridge to the island, then cruised around, easily locating the address and pulling up to the security gate of a waterfront modern glass monstrosity. In this neighborhood, I'd guess the homes to be in the thirty-million-dollar range, give or take a million or ten.

Grey announced himself as Steve Smith, and the gate opened, as did the front door. A short, bald man filled the entry in a black suit. If the air conditioning ever went out, he'd melt. Grey pulled off to the side and parked.

"It would be off-putting to me to have anyone who drives up to the gate be able to see into my house and through to the backyard," I said.

The exterior and lush landscaping were meant to inspire awe, and the water view had immediately caught my attention. Large floor-to-ceiling windows ran across the front and back, and the double front doors were also glass. If there were window coverings, they weren't visible.

"Shouldn't you be carrying for these jobs?" I asked as I got out and joined Grey.

"This is a meet-and-greet, not a shootout."

"Got a great idea — I'll get my concealed carry permit and be your muscle. Cover your back." I pinched his backside, hard.

"Ouch. Dammit," he growled.

"Tsk, tsk, attitude." I put distance between the two of us, hoping to look professional. "Put your party face on, butler dude is staring."

I was surprised when Grey introduced me as Brenda and happy that he didn't use my real name. He didn't offer up a last name, so if asked, I'd go with Jones. Sounded better than Doe. I could already hear Grey groaning.

Butler Dude didn't offer up any kind of greeting. He motioned us to follow him across the immense entry and through the living room, opening the door to a glass-enclosed patio. The room overlooked the water, where the boat dock was currently empty, and a cruise ship was parked across the bay. An older man was huddled on a brown leather couch, a striped pillow stuffed under his head, his scruff of white hair sticking on end, and a blanket wrapped around his shoulders. When the man only stared, Grey made introductions.

"Simon Kent." He waved us to a matching pair of easy chairs, giving me an assessing stare and dismissing me as insignificant.

Everything about this house was oversized, and that included the outdoor living space. The tiered pool took center stage, and the high-end furnishings far outshone what I'd seen on the inside of the house. I snapped my attention back to the conversation as Grey began to ask Mr. Kent questions.

His son, Wilson, sounded like a punk who'd had everything handed to him. Mr. Kent could barely answer a question without coughing and sniffing into his blanket. He picked up the phone and grunted, and the butler reappeared. He was able to decipher the waving of his boss's finger and wrote down Wilson's phone number and handed it to Grey. "When I called, it went to voicemail," Kent muttered. More grunting ensued, and the butler left and returned with a laptop that he handed to Grey.

"Wilson left that behind," Kent croaked, tightening the blanket around his neck.

Before the butler disappeared, I smiled sympathetically at the man, who winked.

Grey opened the laptop and found that it didn't require a password. "You mind if I take this with me?"

Kent waved his hand around. "That's Wilson's personal computer. I had security search his office—they didn't come up with anything—and move his work computer to my office."

"What can you tell me about his friends? Girlfriend?"

Kent shook his head. "The person to ask about that would be Wilson's assistant, Diedre—she always seems to know everything—except she's on vacation for two weeks."

The old goat yammered on, coughing intermittently and barely intelligible, until I wanted to shake him. The man was reputed to be worth millions, but was far too vague in his responses. Hard to believe that he was the one to build the empire. When an answer was required, he kept it short and generic.

My gaze wandered back to the furnishings. I noticed a distinct lack of anything personal sitting out, and that included knick-knacks. One would think there'd be a family photo, something.

Finally, the two men concluded their meeting. I pasted on a smile and stood with Grey. "We'll talk in a day or two." Grey shook the man's hand.

The butler had the patio room door open before we could take step. He led us to the front door, opening it and standing in the entry, then withdrew an envelope from his jacket pocket and handed it to Grey. "As agreed upon with Mr. Kent." He took a step back as we exited, then closed the door.

"You've been in this business a while; are all your client meetings this odd?" I asked once we were away from the house and back at the SUV.

"I've only had one other case where I didn't like the client from the start. Wanted to tell Kent that I wasn't interested, but since I'm starting over, I thought it prudent not to be so choosy." Grey opened the car door for me, and I slid in.

He felt up the envelope before handing it to me. "Didn't think he'd pay in cash. Guess he doesn't want a money trail showing that he hired an investigator." He walked around and slid behind the wheel. "Count it. I asked for a 10K retainer to get started. If it's not all there, your new job will be collections."

Now there's a sucky job. "You'd think Kent, being a businessman, would cut you a check, since it's a legit tax write-off." I upended the bills into my lap as Grey pulled out of the driveway. "Doesn't appear he had to scrape together one-dollar bills." I eyed the hundreds and quickly counted. Twice. "It's a grand short."

"What a cheap f—" Grey made a U-turn. "Kent's power play is unamusing." He pointed at the windshield. "A Mercedes just pulled out of his driveway, and I'm betting it's him." He pulled up to the gate and rang the bell. No answer.

"Interesting that Kent was able to hobble off the couch and get out of the house so fast. If the man isn't straight up enough to pay his bill, you can expect more antics from him. If there's a next time, I volunteer to count the money right in front of him."

Grey drove around the island and checked out the neighborhood of expensive real estate. We didn't pass another car or person out walking. "So Backup, what was your assessment of the meeting?"

"For starters, Mr. Kent is a terrible actor. The sick and feeble act was just that, an act. He put a lot of effort into being evasive. Once or twice, I thought about wandering around outside, checking the pool water to see if it was warm. A more interesting Q&A would've been with the butler."

"I wasn't buying his act either. I'm thinking Kent knows more about the missing money and his criminal son than he was willing to say. Makes me wonder what he was withholding and why he hired me. I'm guessing so he can say he made an effort to find Wilson."

"I'd like to know why Kent thinks the money is recoverable."

Grey merged back onto the Causeway. "My guess is he knows whether or not Wilson has spent every dime or tucked it away somewhere. I'm thinking it might be the latter, since I've been hired to find Wilson and turn him over to Daddy. I had a preliminary background check run, and it showed Wilson's current address as the mansion. Kent never mentioned it and instead gave me an alternative address, clearly wanting me to believe he had no clue where Wilson had gone."

"So Mr. PI, what's the first step?" I asked.

"See if I can track Wilson using his phone or laptop. I'm not sticking my neck out when the client is withholding information." Grey glanced over at me. "Ready for lunch?"

"Raincheck? I have an appointment of my

own. Drop me at home, and I'll grab a burger."

"Hmm…" Grey pulled up to a red light, turned, and stared.

It surprised me that I didn't flinch, but instead returned his stare.

"You're one shifty female."

"That's so mean." I crossed my arms and faux pouted.

"Let's stay on point." His eyebrows went up. "Not one word about this supposed appointment until a minute ago, which means you're up to something or you're full of it. Which is it?"

"I don't like you anymore."

"I'll change your mind later."

I jabbed my finger for him to get off at the next exit. "There's a burger joint to the right. I need an infusion of food and caffeine."

"If you think I've forgotten what we were talking about, you're wrong. Don't think that I won't resort to driving around in circles."

I pulled out my phone and pulled up the address to program the GPS. I didn't really want to go by myself, but he'd flip once he found out what I'd done.

We drove south, exiting into Miami Beach, and pulled into the first burger stand. He went through the drive-thru and ordered for both of us. It surprised me when he circled back around and parked. "I can't believe you allow eating in your pristine ride."

"Just don't throw food all over, and I'll be happy."

"That would be so unladylike," I said, mimicking Gram's tone.

Grey cracked a smile as he pulled out a burger. "Change of plan: we're not leaving here until you tell me what's going on. I'm thinking you're stuck, because it's too far to walk and I'm betting you've never ridden the bus. If there even is one around here. So if you're in a hurry to make your *appointment*, we can eat and talk."

I stuffed the burger in my mouth, buying time. Several times, I'd thought about telling him and chickened out. I'd been rehearsing ways of prettying up the news and had so far come up with nothing. When we finished eating, I'd blurt it out.

We ate in silence.

Grey gathered up the trash, got out, and dumped it. Before getting back in, he stood at the front bumper, pulled out his phone, and had a short conversation. After, he sent a text. Then he got back in and eyed the GPS. "So, where are we going? Is it far from here?"

"Twenty minutes, depending on traffic."

"I'm certain you can impart all the details in that time and leave a few minutes for questions, and if not, just know you won't be getting out of this car."

Chapter Twelve

I turned and stared out the window, another attempt to buy time, and finally turned to face him, sucking in a deep breath. "If you could just keep an open mind…"

"I knew it." Grey banged his hand on the steering wheel.

"You know I've done a lot of research on Mindy's death." I took another breath, this time to calm my jitters. "I located James Slattery." The detective that had originally been assigned to investigate the case. "He's retired now and moved down to the Miami area to be closer to his grandkids."

Grey unleashed a growl or a groan or both at the same time, but otherwise remained silent.

"I called, turned on the charm, and introduced myself as a budding writer. I told him about my interest in the Graham case and asked if he'd answer a few questions."

"Bet he was thrilled."

"In the silence that followed, I implored him, saying that as a first-time author I needed to be certain of my facts, not wanting to write anything untrue and also wanting it to be an authentic account of events." I was getting the silent treatment from Grey. "I went on tell Mr. Slattery that I'd exhausted all my resources for information and wanted to interview people with firsthand knowledge." I admit, I did lead him to believe that I'd already talked to other people.

"You told him you're a first-time author, and he didn't hang up?" Grey looked incredulous.

"Don't be mean."

"I'm doing a lot of that today." Grey unleashed an irritated sigh. "You're telling me that Slattery gets a cold call from a stranger who's poking around in an unsolved murder and agrees to an interview? Just like that?"

"I had to do some fast talking, plead a bit, and promise not to use his name." It didn't escape my notice that Grey's fingers were clenching and unclenching on the steering wheel. "I'm happy that you insisted on coming." More silence. "It's probably not a good idea for you to sit in on the meeting with me. Hang out by the car so Slattery can see that I'm not alone but far enough away that he won't recognize you. Paste on your signature scowl, and from a distance, you'll be sufficiently scary."

"Sounds like a great idea. What you're suggesting is that I stand back and be scary."

I struggled to smile, despite my nervousness. "Exactly."

"You shouldn't be meeting with him at all," Grey snapped.

"I've asked you before and you haven't answered — are you happy being Steve Smith?" No answer. "It would be interesting to hear what Slattery thinks of the case and whether he has any unanswered questions. Does he think you got away with murder?"

The silence was unnerving.

I sighed, accepting that I'd overstepped. "I'll reschedule so you can get started on the Kent case. Better yet, I'll tell the detective that I'm taking his advice and looking for another project."

"Slattery is a straight-up guy. A good detective. He's probably curious to see what you're about. I can't imagine he's had any other calls on the case. But if he's warning you off, you should take his advice."

I stared out the window, wishing that I was swimming in the Atlantic. "Take me home."

"I'll wait by the car, in plain view but unobtrusive. Slattery doesn't have any reason to think I'm back from the dead, or in my case, the never-dead."

"Don't be mad."

"What are your plans for this so-called project of yours?" Grey asked in an even tone, though clearly irked. "Are you just using it as a front, or do you plan on writing this book?"

"I'm only thinking of using it as a cover story — it's a good reason for asking lots of questions and hopefully not raising any eyebrows."

"Who else is on your interview list?"

"In-person interviews might not be the best idea. The next time, I'll see if the person will consent to answering questions over the phone." Grey was probably thinking the same as me— that they'd hang up.

"What about your company?"

"As the owner, my schedule is flexible. I can easily take a day off here and there. As you know, I'm awake early and get everything that needs doing done. Except for something last-minute, I almost always have afternoons free."

"If you're splitting your time, trying to juggle work and investigating, don't you worry that your business will take a hit?"

"I'm not going to let that happen," I said adamantly. "My other motive is the hope that all this sleuthing will pay off and I'll learn a trick or two to help me find my dad." I didn't see any reason to add that staying ridiculously busy kept me from stressing over my dad and Grey. Not to mention that there was a murderer out walking around.

Grey turned off the highway. "Slattery lives in a trailer park?"

"Right, then left, space thirty-nine." I pointed. "I googled the address, and it's got better-than-average reviews. According to the website, it's got all the amenities, pool, tennis, and security."

Grey exited the highway and entered a park-like setting: manicured green grass with plenty of trees. He bypassed two double-wides that had been attached end to end with a sign out front reading "Office," cruised past visitor parking, and took the curve around an inlet of water where a couple of ducks hung out on the bank, searching for food. There were several benches where people could sit and throw bread crumbs at the wildlife while they enjoyed the view. A guard rolled past on a golf cart and waved.

The mobile homes weren't stacked on top of one another—each had a small plot of land and private patio. Grey pulled into the driveway of a turquoise double-wide with white trim and landscaping across the front and parked behind a silver SUV.

The two of us got out, and I leaned back in and grabbed my briefcase. I caught sight of an older man who matched Slattery's description sitting on the lattice-enclosed porch.

Grey and I met at the front bumper. He winked and adjusted his aviators, then grabbed my arm and turned me to face him. "Just be yourself. I'm sure Slattery will be charmed once he figures out you're not conning him on one angle or another."

"I'm really happy you're here." I stood on my tiptoes and gave him a quick kiss. "And that you didn't dump me on the side of the road."

Grey chuckled. "Next time. And I'm certain

there will be one."

As I walked up the driveway, Grey stood off to the driver's side of the car. Slattery, a good-sized man, filled the opening to his patio as he gave me a scrutinizing once-over. I waved and gave him a big smile. "I'm the one that called about the case." I'd given my real first name on the phone but not my last. I'd have to get better at all this subterfuge. "I have a few questions, but I don't want to take up a lot of your time."

Before going inside, he gave Grey a twice-over. "Have a seat." Slattery pointed him to one of the Adirondack chairs that adorned the outside space. Thank goodness they had pillows. "You want something to drink?" He sat with one eye on the driveway.

I shook my head. "I have water in my purse."

"Did you bring my payment?"

"I got the biggest one I could find." I opened my briefcase, pulled out a box of Godiva chocolates, and handed it to him.

"I never thought you'd get so much, but you can bet I'll enjoy every piece." He ran his hand over the top of the gold box and set it on a side table. "Shoot with your questions. A heads up that my grandkids are on the way over, and we won't get a peaceful moment once they arrive."

"Were you convinced Grey Walker was the killer?" I asked, getting right to the point.

"There was no evidence to support an arrest, or we wouldn't have hesitated, cop or not. The body being found on his property wasn't enough, and though he didn't have an alibi for that night, that didn't mean someone else didn't drop her there. Unfortunately for him, the news media convicted him, and for some, that was enough. I did wonder where they were getting their information. They certainly had a lot of it, albeit false." Slattery downed most of his iced tea, then chewed on an ice cube.

"Mindy Graham's journal must have been an interesting twist."

"It was shocking when it came out that a young rich girl who could've chosen any path in life had tried to perpetrate a hoax that would ruin a man's life. Then ended up dead, though that wasn't her intent, according to her own words. There were whispers of suicide — once again the news — but that was quickly disproven. I hated retiring with *any* unsolved cases still on my desk, but this one really rankles."

A little ankle-biter dog bounded out of the house, leaped into Slattery's lap, and made himself comfortable, staring at me. Slattery scratched his head absently.

"There hadn't been any mention of the case in a while... until Detective Walker was found dead. Is there someone still actively working it?"

"Cases stay open until someone is charged. How much attention it's currently getting, I have no idea." He fingered another ice cube out of his glass. "It's my opinion that Mindy's father had the clout to keep the investigation quiet. He told me once that he was tired of seeing his family name on the nightly news. I'd have thought he'd be pushing hard for an arrest." He shook his head. "I was sorry to hear about Walker; thought he got a raw deal. Once your reputation is flushed, it's next to impossible to get it back."

"Did you have any other persons of interest?" I asked.

"We looked at family and friends, for all the good that did. They all lawyered up. And these were people supposedly close to Mindy Graham; you'd think they'd want to be forthcoming and helpful. But nope, they had to be run down and brought in for questioning, and that never turned into anything helpful."

A large white SUV pulled up, the doors opened, and four kids of various ages piled out, all screaming and laughing over one another.

I noticed that Slattery looked relieved by their arrival and glanced furtively at my watch. Ten minutes. It wouldn't surprise me to learn that he'd planned the interruption to happen when it did. I stood. "Thank you for your time."

"A word of advice, young lady," Slattery said in a stern tone as he stood. "In most unsolved cases, and some solved ones, there are unanswered questions. Someone killed Mindy Graham and that someone won't be happy you're poking around. You could end up dead."

I stepped back from the patio opening as the

kids dashed forward and breezed by me, hollering "Grandpa" as they swarmed him for a group hug. I waved and kept walking.

Grey had the passenger door open and didn't take his eyes off me as I approached. Once we were both inside, he asked, "What was in the box?"

"Godiva chocolates that he requested to do the interview."

"I'm certain you didn't get enough info to cover the cost of that box of candy."

Rather than agree, I said, "Now's the time to fess up if you're a sweets-hater. It would be sad to part ways, but better now than later. You know, after you're all broken in and I've got you trained... and then find out you abhor sweets."

Grey laughed. "No worries there, hon."

I took my phone out and sent myself a couple of notes.

"To show you what a great boyfriend I can be..." Grey grinned.

"Boyfriend." I smiled at him.

"Have you broken the news to your friends yet?"

"I'll do it at our weekly breakfast. I can't tell one before the other. I'm certain that neither is going to be surprised." Knowing those two, they figured it out before me. "Back to you proving your greatness..."

"Write down your questions, run them by me, and I'll give you my opinion... which, by the way, is one of my favorite things to do. Also on that list, include the people you plan to contact." Grey raised his brows, as though I'd argue.

Not just yet.

"Early on, I figured out that I would need to keep an eye on you, and that's panned out." Grey pinned me with a stare as he turned onto the highway. "I propose that I be your backup for these sit-downs of yours, and in return, you can help me figure out where Wilson is hiding. That should keep you busy and out of trouble. Hopefully." Grey reached out and clasped my hand. "You'll be great backup, Brenda."

"That's Miss Jones to you," I said in a snooty tone, struggling not to laugh.

Grey laughed. "Smith and Jones, now there's a great name for my new business."

"I'd prefer alphabetical order."

Chapter Thirteen

I followed the scent of freshly brewed coffee into the kitchen and heard Grey tell someone, "I've got his laptop." I eyed it where it sat on the island as I slipped onto a stool. I waited for him to hang up, then banged my hand on the granite. "Coffee."

"Yes, ma'am." He bowed, then picked up a mug, filled it, and set it front of me.

The front door slammed, and Avery poked her head around the corner, large sequined frames today's fashion choice, then danced in barefoot, in jeans, and crossed over to the island, tossing down a large bag.

"You're supposed to knock," I reminded her.

"Since when? Never." She opened a cupboard and took out a plate, then turned the bag upside down, and a variety of donuts fell out.

"You might catch Grey naked, and then you'll feel bad that you don't have such an amazing specimen lurking around your house."

Grey shook his head.

"It's fate that I brought donuts." Avery licked her lips. "Does this mean you two are…" She scissored her fingers and turned her attention to

Grey. "Just trying to get the visual of you in your birthday suit."

I attempted to kick her, and she scooted away, laughing.

Grey poured her a mug of coffee, then set out plates and a roll of paper towels.

Avery eyed the laptop. "Is that the one?"

Grey handed it to her. "I appreciate this. I attempted to snoop through the files last night, but I couldn't find any."

Avery flipped it open. "It's an older model." She clicked around. "People think they're so clever. Someone deleted all the files but forgot to empty the recycle bin, which only means they won't take as long to recover. I can transfer all the information to a drive and get it to you later today."

"I appreciate you helping me out like this," Grey said. "You blew off payment, so just know that if there's anything I can ever do, ask. The answer is, 'I'll get on it.'"

"I love a good mystery." Avery closed the laptop. "So excited about being on the good side of an investigation. Wouldn't feel the same if I was the one under the microscope."

Grey nodded in agreement.

"More." Avery banged her mug on the island.

Grey laughed. He stood and reached for the pot, refilling it for her.

"Interesting news about the phone number you gave me..." Avery said.

"I'm impressed that you've got something for me already." Grey tipped his mug towards her in a toast.

"If someone doesn't want to be found, they should do a little research and learn to turn off their phone and get rid of the battery. The location of the phone is… the mansion. There's an app running on it that disconnects calls after the second ring. I remotely installed an app of my own, and I'm tracking all the calls."

"I wonder who installed that—Kent or Wilson?" Grey mused. "It's hard to believe that there's a phone ringing somewhere in the mansion and that nosey butler doesn't know jack about it."

"Didn't have the time to do a thorough check on the Kent family, but a little digging uncovered a couple of interesting facts." Avery took a big bite out of a jelly donut and savored it with a sigh before continuing. "What surprised me was how unsecure the company computers are… until I noticed that the coffers are being looted. Someone's ripping off the company to the tune of millions. With just a glance, it's hard to know if the culprit is the son. I do know something about corporations, and it's going to come out, probably before the next board meeting. Kent's position is in jeopardy if the money hasn't been returned. If I were a board member, I'd vote to kick him off, especially if he's involved in any attempt to cover it up."

"Would it placate the members if the money were returned before they found out?" I asked.

"I imagine Kent would have to call in every favor ever owed him to keep his seat," Grey answered. "Is it possible to find out if Wilson is the culprit? Or where the money's going, regardless of who's stealing it?"

"Avery's a numbers wizard." I got up and grabbed a water, having met my coffee limit for the day.

"It will take a few days, but I'll be able to track the cash and give you a report covering everything you need to know." Avery grinned at Grey.

"If Kent continues to cover for his son, and he turns out to be the culprit, then he's looking at criminal charges," I said.

"All it would take is one board member finding out and calling the cops. It could become a major case overnight," Grey said.

"Once it hit the news, the stockholders would get screwed. In addition to a securities investigation, there would be criminal charges and, I'm certain, lawsuits from the stockholders," Avery said. "I have a little news on a different subject. I went by the office building yesterday, and the workers were de-ratting the place. I took a quick peek around and left. Hugo says it will be ready by the first of next week."

"The security doors will be installed by then," Grey told her. "Not to be bossy, but... don't be hanging around there by yourself until then, and not at night. Ever. I'm thinking of your safety and that of anyone else that's going to work there. I'm not expecting any trouble, just want everyone to be safe."

"The reason the move into the offices will be delayed by several days is my fault," Avery said with a shifty smile. "I ordered all the offices painted, and Hugo's men are jumping on it."

"The *next* time, do you think you could run it by me first?" I asked.

"That's a familiar question," Grey said, his lips quirked.

"Promise." Avery held up her hand. "It's going to be a big improvement. The faded and yellowed walls will be gone, and it will no longer look like an animal's been lifting its leg."

Eww. "It's a great idea. Glad you thought of it." I smiled my thanks.

"You ready for another great idea?" Avery grinned.

"Twice in one day is too much for me." I almost laughed at her faux outrage.

"You've got to jump on this one. Hugo told me he'd like to rent the first floor. He needs an office for his business, since it's grown and he doesn't want to run it out of his truck anymore. I'm thinking the more hulky guys hanging around, the better. Discourages troublemakers. I told him I'd put in a good word."

I looked at Grey, and he nodded and said, "Not the worst idea."

"It's a good idea…" I trailed off.

"But?" Avery questioned.

"What happens if my dad comes back and there's all these changes?"

"It's not if but when. Since he thinks you're near-perfect, he'll be fine. And when it does happen, I'll sit him down and recommend that he diversify and buy more real estate." Avery's phone dinged; she pulled it out of her pocket and glanced at the screen. "I'm meeting a client." She stood and grabbed the laptop. "I'll get on transferring the files and get it back to you no later than tomorrow." She waved and left.

Grey patted my hand. "When your dad comes back, it's not going to be a problem. I'll move out, and he can have his old office back."

I stood, slid into his arms, and hugged him.

Chapter Fourteen

After Avery left, I cleaned up the kitchen and went out to the balcony, sitting next to Grey. "Are you going to feed me before or after your trip back to Kent's house?"

He gave me a distracted smile, and when he spoke, it wasn't to answer my question. "There's something off about this case. I'm wondering if it's a setup of some kind. Since I don't know the man, I did a little digging online and came up with almost nothing. Perhaps I'm just generally paranoid."

"Have all your other cases been straightforward?"

"There's usually some hurdle that has you wondering what the heck. You regroup and come up with a different angle to approach the problem." Grey heaved a sigh. "I was hired to find Kent's son, and everything points to him being holed up in the mansion. Or someone else is busy on his phone. I find it hard to believe that Kent wouldn't know."

"I get that the house is big, but how could he possibly be living there without either of the other two residents noticing?" I found it hard to believe anything got past the butler. "The first thing that would stick out would be Wilson's car... unless he walked, which I doubt. If Kent's sincere about wanting to find his son, then he won't mind if you have a look around the house."

"I would've asked yesterday if I'd had any indication Wilson lived or stayed there. I googled the address Kent's butler gave me, and it's a mail drop. Another 'what the hell' question for the old guy. I'm assuming Kent's never paid his son a visit."

"Go check out the mailbox place and turn on the charm, flash a little cash, and maybe whoever is behind the counter will break the rules and give you Wilson's address of record," I suggested.

"Maybe... people are sometimes willing to take a chance on making a buck if they think they won't get caught." Grey stood and pulled me to my feet. "Let's go for a ride."

We got in the SUV, and Grey headed straight back to Palm Island, which was a short trip. He drove up to the security gate and hung his head out the window, pressing a button on the panel.

"How can I help you?" The butler's voice came through loud and clear.

I was surprised that he didn't greet Grey by name, since we were just there.

"Steve Smith. I'd like to speak with Mr. Kent."

"Do you have an appointment?"

"I have a few questions that I need answered to move his case forward. It won't take too much of his time."

"Mr. Kent is not at home, and I don't have an exact time for his return," the butler said, rebuke in his tone. "I suggest that before coming back, you call first."

"How about Wilson Kent? Does he have a few minutes?"

Total silence. There was no way to tell if Grey and the butler were still connected.

Finally, the butler came back on. "Wilson doesn't live here. I gave you his address when you were here last."

"Were you aware that that *address* was to a rented mailbox?"

Another long pause. "I had no idea. I'll have to let Mr. Kent know."

I found it hard to believe he was telling the truth. But why lie? Unless he was part of whatever was happening behind the scenes.

"Since I'm here, I'd like to come in and have a look around," Grey said. "I might be able to pick up a clue to facilitate Mr. Kent's case."

Dead silence. Grey's jaw tightened as he waited for the man to respond.

The butler finally came back on. "I'd have to have Mr. Kent's authorization, and as you know, he's not here to ask."

"Have Mr. Kent call me." Grey backed out of the driveway.

"With the delayed responses to your questions, the butler was acting shifty," I said. "Probably following instructions. Be interesting to see how long it takes Kent to call you back."

"*If* he does. Either will be telling. My instincts tell me that there's more going on than Kent's said. No investigator wants to be left in the dark."

"Ender would be the one to ask, since he was the referral," I said.

"When I first considered taking the job, I had a few questions I wanted answered without making it sound like the third degree. Ender assured me that his badass reputation was an exaggeration and he's a straight-up businessman with several ventures going. Due to family connections, he knows everyone, which is how this case landed in his lap."

Ender's father had the same fierce reputation as his son. Lots of whispers and speculation, but no one in the family had ever gone to jail.

"I told Ender that I wasn't interested in anything not on the up and up and that he better be listening, as I wasn't the same puny fellow from elementary school and I'd kick his ass. He laughed." Grey's lips turned up in a half-smile. "I'll give him a call and see what he knows." He picked up his phone and called, hissing at having to leave a message.

"I thought we were headed to the mailbox place," I said as he turned back towards home.

Grey shook his head. "I'm not going to ask for info that could lead to someone losing their job. I'm taking a step back until I figure out what I'm dealing with, and in the meantime, Avery is ferreting out what I hope will be a wealth of information."

Chapter Fifteen

Grey spent the next day stomping around, grunting and growling. He'd left another message for Kent, which went unanswered. Ender had returned his call quickly and promised to get on the phone with his connection and get back to Grey, but that hadn't happened yet.

I suggested that Grey take his frustration downstairs to the gym. He came back a sweaty mess and hit the shower, then came out to the balcony sporting a black t-shirt that molded to his muscles and a pair of sweat shorts. With a laptop and USB drive in hand, he lowered himself into the chair next to me.

Avery had dropped off Wilson's laptop earlier, leaving it on the entry table, a drive with the information she'd procured lying on top.

"Thanks for the gym tip." He leaned over and kissed my cheek. He'd barely gotten the laptop open when his phone rang. He jumped up and went to grab it from the other room.

I hoped it was Ender with some news, but I swore I heard him say Gram. What the heck? If anyone thought it was easy to eavesdrop on one-sided phone calls, they were wrong. Based on Grey's responses, I had no clue what they were talking about or why she would call him. The call didn't last long, and then Grey disappeared down the hall. In a few minutes, he was back, having changed into blue jeans and a dress shirt.

"I'll be back in a few hours." He leaned down and brushed my lips with a quick kiss.

I fisted his shirt. "Hold on a sec." His smirky smile flashed across his face—briefly, but long enough for me to catch it, and go on alert. "What are you doing for Gram? Why would she call you and not me?"

"You were listening?"

"If it was a private conversation, you should've gone into the kitchen and not stood a foot behind me." I closed my laptop and set it on the side table. "Back to Gram." I jumped up.

"Client confidentiality."

"Partner," I hissed. "That would be me."

Grey waved. "See you later."

"Sooner than you think," I yelled as the door banged closed. "Not so fast, buster," I grumbled, then grabbed up my phone and called Gram. No answer. Since when? The woman was married to her phone. I hit redial. No answer. We'd be having a reminder talk about *always* answering her phone. I raced to my bedroom and pulled on a sleeveless sundress, a clam shell belt, and a pair of slides. In between putting on each piece of clothing, I called Gram. Her voicemail would be full of breathing messages.

Grabbing up my purse and keys, I flew out the door. I got down to the garage and skidded to a stop.

Grey stood next to his SUV, the passenger door open. He tapped his watch. "That took longer than I thought. But I didn't factor in you doing a quick change."

I stormed past him and slid onto the seat. "As though I'd go to Gram's in shorts."

Grey laughed and shut the door, then went around and got behind the wheel.

"Reassure me that Gram is okay."

"One of her friends wandered off, and she's worried. He's not supposed to be driving, and she wants me to find him before he gets into 'jail trouble,' as she called it."

"And she called you? Because you're on a friendly basis with all the neighborhood peeps?" This all sounded familiar *and* more reason why Gram should've called me, since I'd helped her with this kind of incident in the past.

"I'm the professional."

"Gram's up to something," I mumbled and leaned back in my seat.

It surprised me that, despite having only been to Gram's once, Grey knew the way and didn't ask for directions. Traffic was on the light side, and we made it faster than usual.

Grey checked in with the guard at the shack, and we were waved in. "Why does your Gram park her collector car in the driveway and not keep it in the garage?" He pulled up alongside the Thunderbird.

"That's her way of saying, 'I'm home.'"

"Really bad idea. I'm going to have a talk with her after I've solved her current problem."

I smiled noncommittally. Good luck. I'd harangued her since she moved in to do just that and see where that'd gotten me. He'd find out on his own that if it garnered Gram more attention to request help, real or not, she'd be calling for help all the time.

By the time we got out, Gram stood in the doorway with a welcoming grin. She wrapped her arms around me in a smothering hug. "I hoped you'd show, proving me right that you're h-o-t for him," she whispered hoarsely in my ear.

If Grey couldn't hear every word, then he needed to get his ears checked.

"Mrs. Winters." Grey leaned over her outstretched hand, kissing the back of it.

"You're to call me Gram, young man." She tittered.

I was too old to be sent to my room for eye-rolling, but I turned away and then did it. Old habits. I left the two fawning over one another and went inside to take a seat, the others right behind me. I needed to get comfortable to hear Gram out. I'd bet she left out a fact or two when she called Grey. It wouldn't take him long to catch on to her tricks, and in the meantime, I'd enjoy the show.

Gram didn't ask but handed us each a glass of iced tea from the tray she'd assembled, then settled on the couch across from us. "Bernard is a dear friend, and I don't want him getting into trouble."

"Nate Bern again?" I asked in surprise. "You're calling Grey when I found him the last time and took his keys away?"

"I know that you're special friends, and don't want to mar the relationship in any way." Gram trotted out her used-car-salesman smile.

"You make it sound like Bern and I have cha-chaed in the past, and that never happened. Besides, he's a hundred if he's a day. I wouldn't want the poor man expiring."

Grey laughed.

"Harper Finn," Gram said in exasperation.

I waved, which made her smile. Using her antics against her was paying off at the moment.

"So, Grey dear…" Gram turned her attention to him. "Bern is a drinker and likes to suck down the sauce. He favors the bars where the servers are half-dressed and have large… well, you know." She pulled a piece of paper out of her pocket and handed it to him. "These are his favorite haunts. I tried calling a couple of them and got put on hold for so long that my ear started to hurt."

"I thought I taught you how to press the speaker button," I said.

"Yes, dear," Gram said absently.

"So you called Grey, who charges a thousand bucks an hour, when I found dear Bern the last time and only got a cold one out of it."

"There's no charge for family," Grey reassured Gram, since she'd stuttered when I mentioned his inflated hourly rate.

Gram preened. "The two of you working together will find Bern that much faster."

"Except you never mentioned me asking Harper." Grey stared at Gram in a way that would make most squirm.

"I know my Harper. No way was she going to miss being in the middle of the action. And look…" Gram waved her hand. "Here she is."

Grey perused the list. "Do you know where these establishments are located?" He handed me the list.

"That's a big five-dollar word for dive bars." I returned Grey's flinty stare. "And yes, I know where they all are, and before you ask, I've been in all of them, but not as a regular."

"You two make such a cute team," Gram cooed.

Grey focused his stare on Gram, brows raised. "Give me a good reason why we're interrupting an old man's fun?"

"Bern and I are friends, and I promised to help him stay on the straight and narrow. Mostly anyway. If you need to play hardball, remind him that if his son gets wind of him getting in trouble, he'll follow through on his threat to move him out of here."

After a quick perusal of the list, I handed it back to Grey. "How about a little contest? Whoever finds Bern first wins bragging rights and can lord it over the other. Loser coughs up for a fancy dinner on the beach."

Grey turned and glared, and I returned a ferocious one of my own, almost laughing. "I hear a setup," he grumbled.

"Now, now." Gram stood. "You two are the cutest. I still haven't heard how you met."

Grey and I exchanged an "I dare you to tell her" look that rapidly changed to "You tell her; no, you do it."

"Since you don't have your ride, I win by default… unless you're taking your Gram's car." Grey looked pleased when Gram hissed.

"Gram doesn't allow anyone else to climb behind the wheel. She can barely stand it when someone occupies the passenger seat." I waved his car keys. "But maybe she'll make an exception for you."

Grey stood and turned his pocket inside out. "That's the second time you've pilfered my pockets. I hate it."

"My girl's got a few crafty tricks." Gram beamed at me and grabbed Grey's arm, then mine, and herded us toward the door.

At the door, I disengaged from Gram's hold and waited at the end of the porch as the other two trailed behind. "What are you really up to?" I asked her.

"He's a keeper, that one." She patted my cheek.

I caught Grey's smirk over her shoulder.

"A little adventure will be fun for your relationship. Show that you're meant to be together." Gram beamed.

"What it's going to show him is that we're a family of nutjobs." I didn't bother to lower my voice, knowing he could hear every word. "For the record, he's already given me that swell nickname. Your antics are only reinforcing that he's right."

Gram grabbed my shoulders, giving them a shake. Grey smirked, enjoying watching the two of us. "You need to show him what a great partner you'd be, and then I'll get the grandchildren I want."

I didn't think my cheeks could burn more than they were at the moment. "Newsflash: we just met."

Gram gave me a slight push forward. "Don't keep Grey waiting. Men don't like that."

I closed the space between Grey and I, and he hooked his arm around me and led me over to the SUV. "Love your Gram." He held out his hand.

"You want the keys?" I took them out of my pocket and unlocked the doors, then handed them to him. "You might as well learn your way around town, since I'm certain there will be more distress calls." I walked around and got in the passenger side, then pulled out my phone.

"Your Gram is quite the matchmaker," Grey said in an amused tone. "I take it she doesn't know we're close?" He honked and waved as he headed to the exit.

"You think you're so funny. You know what they say about the apple... Don't be surprised if the next time you wake from a stupor, we're married. As for Gram, since she's gotten it into her head that you're a keeper, you even hint about our closeness and see how fast we end up in matrimonial bliss."

Grey laughed.

"Following Gram's advice, I'm supposed to show you how useful I can be." My mouth twitched up in a smile. "Forget the list and head to Captain's. It's a hole in the wall and only a couple of miles straight down the road. It's a colorful shack that caters to locals—mostly men who like to be fawned over by big-busted, scantily clad women—and, in my opinion, a waste of prime real estate."

"You were going to win the challenge with inside knowledge?" he asked in a shocked tone.

The man was a good actor, I'd give him that. I didn't feel the least bit guilty, since I knew he'd been entertained by Gram's antics. "Calm your horses, as Gram would say. I'm proposing that we both get a trophy for our team effort. I've done my part. Now you pokey on into Cap's and haul Bern out. I'll wait in the car." I trotted out the shiftiest smile I could manage. "Another tip: partners and all…" I ignored his snort. "You need to come up with a good bribe, or you'll be dragging his scrawny backside to the car."

"What about his car?"

"You get him back to the car, and I'll relieve him of his keys and drive it back."

"You're way too good at pickpocketing." Grey shook his head. "I hope you're not practicing on just any Joe that stumbles by."

"Just friends." I pointed. "That dirt patch within spitting distance is the parking lot."

Grey pulled into the gravel lot and parked. He hung his head over the steering wheel, staring at the brown wood-sided shotgun-style building splashed with various colors of paint, a red ramp up to the double glass doors. At first glance, one would think it was a dank hole, and they'd be right. But Cap did a brisk business, as evidenced by the half-dozen cars parked haphazardly in the lot.

"You coming?" Grey opened the door.

"You want me to wave my girls under his nose, get him moving?" I demonstrated.

Grey growled and shut the door.

I guess not. I laughed, got out, and leaned against the front bumper. Normally I'd want to be in the middle of the action—clearly it was in the DNA—but I'd been in there before, and the smell of animal pee was too much for my sensitive nose. I'd held my nose the last time and earned a glare from Cap himself.

It took longer than I expected, but Grey and Bern finally came out, chumming it up like old friends. Bern looked my way and did a double take. I waved, walked over to meet them, and held out my hand. "Keys, dude."

"I love it when you talk all sexy." Bern held up his hands. "Go ahead and feel me up."

"You need to behave yourself." I hugged him, then straightened and stepped back. "I'll see you two back at the house." I jingled the keys as I strutted over to a baby blue rust bucket, the front hood about eaten through.

"I'm going to marry her," Bern cooed.

Grey snorted and asked, "What is that and does it even run?"

"Have some respect for Gracie." I patted the roof of the car. "She's a 1966 Porsche 912 and runs like a dream. Bern's promised that when he's ready to sell, I get to make the first offer."

"You're sure it won't break down?" Grey eyed it suspiciously.

Bern snorted and attempted to slug Grey in the arm, but ended up tripping over his feet. Grey caught him before he hit the dirt.

"Don't you listen to him, Gracie." I stuck my hand in the rolled-down window to open the door. I hopped in and shifted around in the sunken seat, getting the springs just right where I could still see over the steering wheel. "Gracie, when you're mine, I'm tricking you out. Not a speck of rust for you, babes."

I followed Grey out to the highway, then put it in gear and blew by him, honking and waving. Soon, they were a speck in my rearview mirror, and I roared back to Gram's, the breeze blowing through the windows keeping me from expiring in the heat.

Chapter Sixteen

I waved to the guard as I blew past, parked Gracie in Bern's garage, and with one last wave to the car, locked her up. Then I removed the ignition key from the ring and stashed it on one of the shelves over the work space that never saw any action.

Ender lumbered over in jeans and a t-shirt that barely fit across his chest, showing off his thick, muscled arms, and met me at the end of Gram's driveway. "What kind of trouble is Bern in?"

"None for now. He was out driving around when he shouldn't be. Grey's bringing him back."

"Bern needs to offload that piece of —"

I cut him off. "You need to have some appreciation."

"Yeah, okay." Ender looked around. "I've got an update for Grey on the Kent case, one he's probably not going to like."

"He'll be driving up any second. If this case has red flags, you need to give him a heads up. He's got a lot on the line."

Ender gave me a hard stare, letting me know he didn't like being told what to do.

"In case you hadn't heard, I went with him to the mansion, and I know Kent's full of it. If he doesn't have anything to hide, he didn't act like it."

Ender made kissy noises. "Who knew you could make a go of a relationship with the man."

"Grow up," I said with a shake of my head. "If it's any of your business, we're growing on one another."

"I should've known you wouldn't just go on a dating app and meet someone I could scare the daylights out of if he crossed you." Ender grinned at the SUV approaching. "How is it that you beat him back here?"

"Grey drives the speed limit." I laughed at Ender's snort. "He's got Bern in the car, and I'm guessing they made a liquor store run. Knowing the old guy, he got that concession before he got in the car."

"I don't know why Bern goes off the property when every oldster here has a well-stocked liquor cabinet, not to mention the beach bar and restaurant." Ender flicked his finger around. "Stand back…" He turned as Gram's front door opened and she hustled to stand with us in the driveway. "I swear, if she's not lurking in the window, she's got a camera. My granny's the same way."

"I hope I'm around when *Granny* finds out that's what you're calling her behind her back. That stick-skinny woman is going to knock you on your massive behind."

"Not happening." Ender laughed. "I'll run. When I show back up, it will be with enough sweets to last her a year."

Grey parked in the driveway and got out holding a three-bottle cardboard carrier. He attempted to hand it off to Bern, who brushed it away for a hug from Gram, who was admonishing him like an errant teen. He squeezed her hard, and she squeaked. End of lecture.

Bern hooked his arm around Gram, and they headed off down the street.

"Neither of you has permission to go very far," I yelled.

They both waved over their heads, neither breaking stride.

Grey dropped the liquor purchase inside the house and joined Ender and I, leaning against the rear of his Escalade. "You got anything for me?" he grouched as he got closer.

"Bern work your last nerve?" I asked.

"One would've thought he couldn't get through another day without his whiskey and tequila. I told him I'd stop on the condition of no more drinking and driving." The irritation rolled off him.

"No worries. I hid the ignition key, so next liquor run, he can call an Uber."

Grey hooked an arm around me. "Kent's not returning my calls," he told Ender.

"Here's the deal. The CFO is an acquaintance of mine and is the one that called for a referral to an investigator, hence how you got involved. He noticed the missing money and warned Kent that he better get it back in the account before it was discovered, became a legal issue, and the stock tanked."

"How did Kent take the ultimatum?" Grey asked.

"About like you'd expect—blew it off." Ender's face conveyed that Kent was stupid. "My friend, not wanting any blowback landing in his lap, confided in a board member. The two of them cornered Kent, planning to pressure him into returning the money from his personal account if the son had spent it and then force both their resignations. Kent could retire, and no one would be the wiser."

"Wouldn't that require some creative accounting?" I asked.

Ender shot me a look that clearly said, *No one's asking you.*

"Why did Kent hire me if he wasn't going to be cooperative? Not to mention pay a sizeable retainer for dick-around privileges."

"Kent put on a good show about wanting Wilson found, but it was a ruse. Wilson took off to the Caribbean, where the family owns a house, and there's no way the old man doesn't know. The security guard on the property would've called. If Wilson thinks there's no extradition for monetary crimes, he didn't do his homework."

"That says to me that Kent is buying time. But for what?" Grey asked.

"Just the fact that he hired you makes him look proactive," Ender said.

I threw in my two cents. "Or he's looking for a way to put the blame on Grey."

"Speaking of scapegoats..." Ender said. "My friend thinks Kent stole the money and is putting the blame on his kid. I met the kid once; he's a worm. When the cops catch up to him, he'll sell out whoever he has to to avoid jail. True or not." With an apologetic look, he added, "I honestly thought this was a straightforward case. It didn't implode until after I got you involved."

"I'm going to tell the old guy to stick the job," Grey said.

"Hold off on that. Don't contact Kent. Let's see how this plays out."

"I'll let you know if he returns my calls, but I'm thinking that probably won't happen."

Chapter Seventeen

It was the start of a new week, and there'd been no calls from Kent. Grey hadn't tried to get in touch since his conversation with Ender, and there'd been no new updates from the man.

The offices were ready for occupancy. Avery presented Hugo with an exhaustive punch list, and he put his guys on it and got everything done in short order. Thanks to a connection of Hugo's, the elevator was now working.

It would be an easy move for Grey, since he planned to use the desk and chairs already there, but he hadn't shown any interest since he started working from my home office. Avery hired a moving van, which packed up her previous office space and hauled everything upstairs.

It was early, and I was awake and dressed in a knee-length dress and low heels. I went in search of coffee and found Grey with a fresh pot brewing.

Grey whistled as I walked into the kitchen. "It's a little early for an appointment."

"Not if it's in Orlando and I need to be there by noon." His blue eyes turned chilly, and I braced myself for an irritated response. "Even though I'm dressed and ready to leave, if after I tell you the plan for the day, you strongly object, I'll call and cancel."

Grey mumbled something under his breath. "I *thought* our agreement was for you to discuss things with me before going off half-cocked. Did I misunderstand?"

"I object to your description. That said, technically I am giving you a heads up."

"Are you always on the lookout for a loophole?" Grey shook his head. "I'm afraid to ask who you're meeting."

"I got Jeff Graham to agree to meet me."

"Mindy's father?" His tone was clearly skeptical. "Surprised you could get him on the phone."

"I used a friend-of-a-friend, twice-removed connection."

"I'm going to tell that damn Ender to stop helping you. I'd threaten to kick his oversized butt but would need to hire someone from the WWF to do it."

I didn't bother to tell him that it wasn't Ender. "You have options here."

"I'm pretty certain that I know what they are, but why don't you enlighten me?"

"We don't have time for a detailed discussion, so tell me to butt out or hurry up and change, and while you're driving me to my appointment, I'll go over all the deets."

Without a word, he headed down the hall. I heard the shower and took it as a sign that he was coming with me.

We were headed north on the Turnpike when he said, "So you called Graham, and he said, 'Sure. Come on over,' to a total stranger? Who does he think you are? More importantly, what does he think you want?"

"I introduced myself as Brenda Jones, budding writer, and said that I was researching his daughter's murder and wanted my account to be factual. I also said that if I uncovered any new information, I'd be happy to share."

"That's nervy."

"Graham thought so too. When I asked if he'd meet with me, he told me to butt out and hung up." I'd been mortified and stared at the phone, wishing I could take the call back. "To my surprise, shock, and a host of other emotions, he called back and agreed to a meeting."

"Interesting turnaround," Grey grumped.

"Or… maybe after some thought, he decided he wanted a fair representation of his daughter's story."

"Who chose the location?"

"Graham texted the address, which I googled. According to the picture, it's a coffee shop with an outdoor patio. If we get there ahead of him, I'm going to get a table outside where I have a view of both inside and out."

"You're not to go anywhere with him, no

matter what he says. I won't be far away, and if you think the conversation is getting out of hand, get up and leave, and I'll be right beside you, telling him to take a hike."

"You think I can expect trouble?"

"I just think his about-face is odd. It's possible that he just wants some input into the project, but what else?" Grey shook his head. "When I checked into his background, he came back squeaky clean, and I couldn't find anyone with a bad word to say about the man." We lapsed into silence and were almost to the turnoff when Grey asked, "What are you going to ask him?"

"I don't want to be too invasive. I'm going to introduce myself and tell him that I became interested in the case, followed the extensive news coverage, and it inspired me to write a book." My supposed great idea was now making me squirm at the thought of the face-to-face about to happen. "I'm interested to know if he thinks that his daughter's murderer is dead or believes there's someone still walking around."

"And did you follow the case?" Grey asked.

"You know I didn't. I only researched and read everything I could find after the order to off you came in."

"You've been wanting an answer from me on whether I want my name cleared, and the answer has always been yes. But not if something happens to you."

I reached out and squeezed his hand.

"Not to be discouraging…" There was a 'but' in Grey's voice. "You could interview everyone connected to the case and not come up with a viable suspect. It's already been done by law enforcement, and trust me, they were thorough. And if the real killer were to get wind of your project, they'd kill you… or attempt to anyway."

"You need someone to ask questions for you. And with you by my side, or close by anyway, I'll be safe."

Grey groaned.

"You could head up your own investigation, since you're the experienced one. But it would require you to out yourself as alive, and that's out of the question. Because…" I aimed my fingers and shot up the car, then let my head drop to my shoulder. Finally, a laugh.

"I'm certain I need a therapist, but not sure how I'd explain you."

"I wouldn't waste time thinking about that. Just revel in the fact that you're the sane one." Another laugh. I wanted to sigh with pleasure. "Until we clear your name, there's no reason you can't be Grey Walker for a select few and Steve for the rest, or another cool moniker. A lot of people in South Florida use one and never advertise their real name. That way, you're not doing anything illegal."

"I've been slow to wrap my head around everything that's happened… just sort of coasting on autopilot, but now I'm kicking my own butt into action."

Grey pulled off the freeway and cruised through town, easily finding the coffee shop in a trendy strip mall. He drove by slowly, and I kept my neck craned but didn't see anything out of the ordinary.

"I'll drop you off a couple of businesses down the sidewalk and go back and park across from the entrance. When you're ready to leave, I'll follow at a discreet distance and pick you up in front of the same store. Or I can get a table and eavesdrop. Either way, I won't be taking my eyes off you."

"Not that I think you're that recognizable…" I eyed his beard, which had grown a bit longer and suited him. "…but since this is your old stomping grounds, maybe you should stay in the car. I wouldn't want someone to make the connection. Drop me at the ice cream store and pick me up at the same place."

Grey coasted to a stop at the curb. "If, for any reason, you feel the least bit uncomfortable, get up and leave." He picked up my phone. "I called myself," he said and handed it back. "Keep it on. Graham does anything untoward, and I'll swoop in and rearrange his face." He leaned across the console and kissed me.

I got out and checked out the flavors of ice cream through the window before proceeding to the coffee shop. Grey U-turned and found a space in front. Not seeing Mr. Graham, I went inside and got an iced coffee. On the way back outside, I found him sitting on a stool at a countertop that looked out the window. Not sure how I missed him on the way in, but he had a coffee sitting in front of him, so he'd been here for at least a short time.

As I approached, I pasted on what I hoped was a friendly smile and introduced myself, thankfully not forgetting my pseudonym, which I had to admit I was enjoying.

"Let's go outside." Graham stood and held the door open.

We had our pick of tables, since it was hot out. Except for one. Grey had decided to move closer and sat at a table at the far end of the patio, his head shoved inside a magazine. I'd ask later where the heck he got it. I was happy that Mr. Graham had suggested that we move outside, since the inside was packed and we might be overheard. I picked a table with a large umbrella.

"I want to thank you for meeting with me," I said, sitting down.

Graham reached in his pocket, pulled out a slip of paper, and slapped it down. It was a blank check. "Name your price. The only reason I agreed to this meeting was to buy you off." He withdrew a pen from his pocket. "I don't want a book written about my daughter and the events all dredged back up again."

My cheeks flamed. I felt like the worst human ever. "I'm sorry," I stuttered. "I'm not taking your money. I'll find something else to write about."

"You don't know the toll this has taken on my family. I've got two daughters at home to think about, and I want them to have some happiness, not have this hanging over their heads." The sadness on his face twisted my heart. "My wife died shortly after my daughter. She was out late, driving too fast, and skidded off the highway."

"I'm sorry," I said softly.

Graham scrutinized my face. "You're not the hardened reporter I was expecting, doing whatever it takes to dig up dirt and make the story an endless headline again."

"I'm sorry. It wasn't my intention..." I didn't know what to say, since I hadn't thought it through past getting answers to help Grey. He stared, waiting for me to finish. "Could I ask one question, and then I'll leave?"

A riot of emotions raced across his face, and it took him so long to answer, I thought he wouldn't. "Go ahead."

"Do you think Grey Walker was the killer?"

"Despite the news reports, I never thought he did it. I was even more sure he wasn't at fault when I found Mindy's journal. It was a hard read." His jaw tightened. "My daughter had mental health issues her entire life. I'd tried to get her help, but my wife disagreed, always brushing off her erratic behavior, insisting that she'd grow up and miraculously stop blaming others for things she'd done herself. No matter how many times I've been over what happened, I can't change anything. What I can do is concentrate on giving my daughters the best life possible and not let anything get in the way." He pulled the top off his pen and moved the check closer. "I'm going to make this out to you."

"You can do that, but I'll tear it up," I said in a firm tone. "I need to take a good look at myself after this. I'm already horribly embarrassed."

"I do not want to go down this road again." His voice unyielding. "I don't want to relocate my family, but I will if I have to."

"You have nothing to worry about from me. I promise you, the project is dead."

"Mr. Graham." A twenty-something stood in front of the table in silk shorts and a shirt. "Haven't seen you in a while. How have you been?" He dragged a chair over and sat down, staring at me as though expecting an introduction.

I pasted on a smile and looked away.

"Rally. Yes, it's been a while." Graham noticed his attention on the check and covered it with his hand. "Hope your family is doing well."

"Everyone's fine."

"If you wouldn't mind, this is a business meeting." Graham arched his brow. "If it's important, give me a call."

If looks could kill… Rally finally stood and stumbled out of the chair. "Our families should get together." His words rang with insincerity. He turned and flashed me an ugly stare, then scurried inside the coffee shop.

I wondered if he planned to order something and hang around until we left.

"I suppose it would have been good manners to introduce you, but he's not someone you want to know." Graham kept his voice low. "He's a neighbor and was a friend of Mindy's. They didn't bring out the best in each other." He shot a glance at the shop window.

"Not that you need my advice, but I'd start practicing your excuse for why you can't attend the dinner."

Graham laughed. "That felt good. My daughters would flip if I accepted. They think he's creepy."

"Thank you for meeting me, even though it was the last thing you wanted to do," I said with sincerity. "I give you my word that I'm moving on to a new project. I've realized that I'm not cut out for this. Your daughters are lucky to have a dad who's thinking about their happiness in such a sad time." I grabbed my purse, and we both stood.

"Let me walk you to your car."

"I saw a dress in a window down the way that I want to go check out." I smiled, feeling my cheeks pinken.

Graham chuckled and held out his hand. We shook.

"It was nice meeting you."

"Same here." He escorted me to the sidewalk, and we went our separate ways.

I turned and scanned the sidewalk back to the coffee shop to see if Rally had followed us, the thought of his eyes all over me creeping me out. He appeared to have left. I didn't break stride and went inside the store that had caught my eye earlier. As I slid my phone out of my pocket, the saleswoman who was about to approach me smiled and turned away. "You still there?" I asked Grey, noting that the screen still showed us as connected.

"As soon as Graham pulls out, I'll pick you up."

I hung up and, after a last glance around, walked back outside and met Grey, who was pulling up to the curb. I got in, breathing a sigh of relief.

"For a damn awkward situation, I could tell that Graham left with no hard feelings," Grey said, admiration in his tone.

"Did you recognize the creepy guy that crashed our conversation?" I asked.

"Rally Charles, trust fund brat from a mega-bucks family. Ran into him once, and he let me know that I was guilty as hell and would get mine."

"What did you say?"

"Ratcheted up a menacing tone and told him to get out of my face before I beat the hell out of him. He ran. Before he did, I told him never to speak to me again. It was a satisfying moment. He called 911, but it didn't go anywhere. I'm sure that, self-entitled a-hole that he is, he talked down to the officers responding, and they probably couldn't have cared less."

"I was happy when Graham got rid of him, which I don't think he expected."

"I kept an eye on Rally. He walked through the coffee shop and out the other exit. I stayed vigilant, and he didn't circle back around." Grey maneuvered into a long line of cars waiting to turn out of the shopping area. "Rally's a blowhard, used to throwing Daddy's name around and getting what he wants."

"I felt unclean, reopening Mr. Graham's wounds. I'm happy to do anything you need to figure this out, but this is my last interview. Maybe."

Grey's head snapped around. "Who else?"

"The only person left on my list is your old partner, Seven. If I get up the courage to give him a call, I'll tell you in advance. Probably another person who'd prefer I get lost."

"I regret that I didn't stay in touch with Seven. Nothing personal, but I doubt he'd speak to you about the case."

Grey stopped at the gas station and filled the tank, and grabbed us cold waters. I changed seats with him and got behind the wheel. I programmed the GPS and took a back road to stay out of traffic and was about to merge onto a toll road when the Escalade took a hard hit. The SUV rocked from side to side, and my head hit the passenger window. Hard. The air bags exploded. I caught a glimpse of an oversized silver pickup in the side mirror. I groaned and took a deep breath as we rolled off the side of the road and into a ditch.

"You okay?" Grey demanded in a fierce tone, pushing the deflated bags out of our faces.

I fingered my temple gingerly. "I'm fine. I think."

"Don't move. I'm calling an ambulance."

"Nooo." I attempted to unbuckle my seatbelt and sucked in a sharp breath. "I'm fine."

I heard a door close, and then mine opened. Grey unfastened my seatbelt and lowered the seat. "You're not. A large bruise is already forming on the side of your head, and there's a laceration across your neck from the seatbelt."

Sirens wailed in the distance. A cop car pulled up, lights flashing.

"I'm worried about you," I whined.

"We have nothing to worry about. They'll take a report, the car will be towed, and we'll be on our way. But first, the hospital."

Another cop car pulled up.

"What happened?" one of the cops demanded.

"Rear-ended by a silver Ford F750, steel bars across the front," Grey told the officer. "Deliberately side-swiped me, rammed me into the ditch, then took off."

"You get any part of the license number?"

Grey shook his head. "Standard Florida tags, that's it."

The cop moved to my side. "You should never move an accident victim; you don't know the extent of their injuries."

"I'm fine," I insisted. "Hit my head, and trust me, it's hard."

The cop smiled.

The ambulance arrived, and the paramedics took over. I was about to argue when Grey cut me off. "Don't listen to her. Much to her surprise, she's not invincible and needs to be checked out."

They agreed with Grey, listening more to him than me. They strapped me down on a stretcher and loaded me in the back of the ambulance.

"I won't be far behind," Grey said as they shut the doors.

Funny guy. This was ridiculous. I wanted to ask for an aspirin or a double shot of caffeine, but I imagined that both requests would be scoffed at.

It didn't take long before we rolled up to the emergency room at the local hospital and I was rolled into a cubicle. A friendly nurse took my vitals and told me the doctor would be in soon. I don't know how long it took, as I dozed off, and when I opened my eyes, a young doctor was checking me over, asking questions, all of which

I answered. I was rolled off for a scan; the tech smiled encouragingly, which I took as a good sign. When I was rolled back to my cubicle, I smiled at Grey, who was waiting for me.

"Sorry I couldn't get here sooner. Even with everyone going out of their way to accommodate me, it took a while, and thankfully no one recognized me." Grey pulled a chair up to the bedside and brushed a kiss on my cheek.

"You're here now." I clasped his hand. "I'm fine."

The doctor strolled in, a smile on his face. Good news. The tests came back normal. My hard head was still intact. No dents or other damage. Once the paperwork was processed, I'd be released.

"I got us a hotel for the night," Grey told me. "Its biggest attraction is it's close by."

"I want to go home," I whined.

"It's late and a long drive."

"The accident was a hit-and-run?" I asked. Grey nodded, his face filled with anger. "I don't know why people don't stop. When they get caught, they're only in more trouble."

"Most people operate under the illusion that they'll never get caught."

Chapter Eighteen

We'd spent the night in a local hotel, but neither of us slept well and were eager to get back on the road. Grey rented a car and took the same route, slowing to check out where the accident had happened before speeding on.

I was happy to be home, even though surly Grey stood in the doorway, threatening severe retribution if I got out of bed. "That wasn't doctor's orders," I told him. "He said to pass on running a marathon."

Grey snorted.

"I'm at least moving out to the balcony. Sitting in the fresh air is what I need. A walk on the beach would also work wonders, you old stick in the mud."

Grey scooped me up and carried me outside, then went back inside and came out with a bottle of my favorite iced tea and my laptop. He dropped into the seat next to me.

The front door banged closed, followed by laughter.

"Don't your friends ever knock?" Grey asked in a grouchy tone.

"You'll have to be patient and give them time

to get used to me getting lucky."

He smirked and leaned his head back. "What do you suppose they're doing in the kitchen?"

"Not cooking, that's for sure." I cupped my hands around my mouth and yelled, "We're out here."

The slider opened at the other end of the balcony. Avery stuck her head out and waved. Rella squeezed past her and set a bakery box and a small shopping bag on the table. Avery disappeared and came out with plates and silverware.

As always, Rella was dressed flawlessly in a bright-yellow fitted sundress and heels, not a blond hair out of place. Avery was in a knee-length University of Miami football jersey and her favorite sneakers.

"Not sure you deserve a special treat, since you broke the girlfriend code and didn't call." Rella leveled a disappointed look at me. "Your... he did." She pointed at Grey.

"The word you're looking for is boyfriend." Grey grunted and offered me his arm. I stood, and we joined the two women at the other end of the balcony.

I sniffed at the box.

Rella pushed me away. "Behave yourself." She opened the box and lifted out a cheesecake, setting it in the center of the table. "All your faves. It's key lime with a graham cracker crust." She reached in the bag and pulled out a can of whipped cream and a container of fresh raspberries.

I licked my lips. "So very sweet of you."

Avery decorated the plates and handed them to Rella, who put a generous slice of cheesecake on each and served it to us.

I took a bite. "Yum," I gushed.

"Grey assured us when he called that you wouldn't be needing major surgery and he'd have you back home late-morning, and here you are." Rella smiled at me.

"Just a little head-banger. I'm fine," I said and absently patted my forehead. I was happy that I'd had Grey arrange a conference call to tell both women about the accident at the same time. They'd had a hundred questions, which he answered patiently.

"Any arrests yet?" Avery asked around a mouthful of decadence.

Grey shook his head. "Unfortunately, I didn't get the plate number off the truck, and with those bars, it may not have any damage, which will make it difficult, if not impossible, to find."

"It's more important that the two of you are okay." Rella smiled at us. "What were you doing in Orlando? Grey said something vague about business."

I told them about my meeting with Graham.

"You approved this scheme of Harper's?" Avery asked Grey, a slight edge to her tone.

"It took a while for me to warm up to the

idea." Grey shot me a sidelong glance.

"You'll all be happy to know I'm giving up the book ruse." I grimaced, remembering the uncomfortable moments with Graham. "I'm going to give one hundred percent of my attention to my business. Except for occasionally poking my nose into what Grey's doing."

Grey laughed. "It's clear that I need to keep an eye on Harper at all times. As you both already know, she gets an idea and runs with it."

"I don't want you digging around and ending up hurt." Avery covered my hand with hers.

"I second that." Rella fist-bumped the two of us.

"Good news," Avery said with a big smile. "I'll be seeing my first client in my new offices on Monday. I snagged a couple of Hugo's men, and they helped move furniture around."

"Your foundation keeping you busy?" I asked Rella.

"You know me—if I don't have a million projects on my desk, I feel like I'm slacking off. I've got a couple new charities that I'm getting ready to sign off on," Rella bubbled with enthusiasm. "I'm planning a fundraiser with one of the charities that I work with. It'll provide funding for children who have cancer and don't have insurance or the means to pay for treatment."

"You're an amazing woman," I said sincerely. "No doubt you'll raise a ton of money."

"How's Mobster taken to you invading his territory?" Rella asked Grey with a grin.

"The other night, I woke up and he was asleep on my foot. I consider that a big step up from him taking a chunk out of my toe." Grey laughed.

"How's the stock market doing? Making your clients richer than they ever imagined?" I asked Avery. "I'm counting on you making me a trillionaire."

Avery whistled. "That's ambitious." She clearly liked the idea. "You know I could talk your ear off about what to buy, sell, and hang onto right now."

I gave serious thought to licking my plate and compromised by running my finger across it several times to make sure I got everything.

"You can have another piece," Rella said in an admonishing tone.

"I wish I had the room." I rubbed my stomach. "You guys are the best."

"What better way to celebrate your good health than with an overload of sweets?" Rella stood and cleaned up the table, taking everything into the kitchen. Coming back, she said, "I have to get to the office." She bent down and kissed my cheek. "Good luck getting her to behave," she said to Grey.

Avery stood and stretched. "I've also got a busy day." She hugged me from behind, and the two walked out together.

Chapter Nineteen

"You've got great friends." Grey's phone rang, and he flashed the screen at me: Mr. Kent. "Took him long enough," he grumbled, then answered with a grunted, "Smith."

Mr. Kent did all the talking, Grey occasionally nodding with a look of disgust on his face.

"You'll need to send me an email officially terminating our relationship." After a pause, Grey said, "If I'd known that, I could've cleared my schedule for today." He hung up and turned to me. "It was all a misunderstanding."

"What was?" I asked.

"Finding his son," Grey said in disgust. "Kent didn't elaborate, just said that my services were no longer needed and to subtract any expenses from the upfront payment and refund the rest."

"You should've told the man you don't do refunds, especially not since you put time into the case."

"I'll itemize the bill, and he can accept it or not."

"No whiff of what's going on?"

Grey shook his head. "Interestingly, during

the conversation, there wasn't a cough out of the man, so he's completely better." He made another call, and based on the number of grunts, I'd bet he was talking to Ender. That was confirmed when he said, "Kent just fired me. You happen to know anything about that?" After a long pause, he added, "Let me know if you hear anything." He hung up, and his phone rang almost immediately. He glanced at the screen, and this time, he walked into the kitchen. I got up and grabbed my laptop, sinking into the closest cushioned chair and propping up my feet.

"Ender's got a job for me," Grey said as he walked back out the patio doors. "I've got to go meet with the fire inspector on a property he owns. You need me to bring you anything?"

"Don't worry about me." I gave him the sneakiest smile I could muster.

He stared at me like I was criminal and he hadn't decided if he was arresting me or not.

I changed tactics and smiled sweetly.

He took my laptop, setting it on the table, scooped me into his arms, and carried me into the bedroom, where he dumped me on the bed before going into the closet.

Now I was worried that my shiftiness had pushed him over the edge and he was about to tie me to the bed. I was about to make a run for it and lock myself in the bathroom when he came out with a black sundress in his hand and tossed it at me.

"If you're not dressed by the time I am, you'll go naked." Grey huffed. "It's not that I don't trust you to stay home and out of trouble, but I don't." He banged the bathroom door closed.

I grinned and hustled into a change of clothes. "Pick me out a pair of flat shoes," I yelled.

He stuck a pair of navy shoes out the door.

I turned up my nose. "Those don't go."

"Then go barefoot."

I spied a pair of black flats under a chair and retrieved them with time enough to sit back down on the edge of the bed and work on being the picture of innocence when Grey came out, dressed in his signature jeans and dress shirt.

He came to a halt, scrutinizing me. "What are you up to now?"

"I'm sitting here. Dressed, by the way." I waved my hand up and down myself.

He handed me my purse and picked me up, carrying me to the elevator.

"I can walk," I grumbled.

"You can also run off. If I have to chase you, I'll be late."

I didn't want to laugh, but I did. He wasn't amused.

When we got in the car, I told him, "I'll do whatever you need me to do."

"Glad to hear it. I've got your role figured out. I'll detail it for you when we get closer."

That meant he didn't have a plan. Be interesting to see if he came up with one or had to fess up that he was full of it. "What's this job about?"

"Ender loaned an investor money to buy and flip a house. The man got behind on his payments."

I winced, knowing the interest would skyrocket from its already exorbitant rate.

"Ender called the loan," Grey continued. "Two nights later, the house burned down. Ender needs to know if there's a whiff of arson. If so, the insurance won't pay and he'll have to rebuild himself or sell for land value. If the latter, he loses money."

"Why isn't he pestering the fire inspector himself?" How often had he bragged that he knew everyone?

"He's got a lot going on right now, making time for a client that wants to borrow a bundle of money at his screw-you interest rates. He claims that if it works out, it will be the start of a money-making partnership. I could hear him salivating over the phone."

"Happy I missed that." I scrunched up my nose. "Ender does get overly excited when talking about money."

"Did you know that he's taking the bar exam?"

"What I know is that he's been going to night school forever. He never talks about his legal ambitions and doesn't invite questions, so it's hard to know anything that goes on with the man." A couple of times, I'd almost laughed when he'd walked away after I hit him with questions about what he was up to. I interpreted that as *mind your own business*. "Any clue what he plans to specialize in?"

"I asked and didn't get a straight answer, but before he changed the subject, he said, 'You need a lawyer, give me a call.'"

"I've never heard of a 'jack of all trades' lawyer. You can't know everything, despite what some people think." I stared out the window, trying to figure out where we were headed, already ready to turn around and head back.

"I hope you're not pointing fingers at my sex."

I pushed my cheeks together and made a face at the reflection in the window before turning back. "Even though I've known Ender for what seems like forever, I had Avery run a background check on him. There are lots of thuggish stories about him, and I wanted to know if they were true."

Grey looked at me: *And.*

"No criminal record. And he filed all the necessary documents to make his corporation legit."

Grey had driven across town and now turned into an older neighborhood, in which the burned-out shell of a house was an eyesore. Good thing it sat in the middle of a large lot, making it harder for the fire to jump to the houses on either side... which it hadn't done. Not even close, based on the burn marks on the grass. The fire department got kudos for responding in record time and keeping it from getting out of control.

"You might as well tell me how you plan to utilize my talents before fire personnel roll up." I did a good job of keeping the smirk out of my tone.

Grey took off his seat belt and turned to me. "You're going to sit here and not do a damn thing. Keep your eyes peeled for any activity in the neighborhood, if you must."

"Like that woman walking her dog." I pointed at the duo headed our way.

"Adjust your seat back, roll down the window, let the heat roll in. That'll be fun."

"If that's your attempt at humor, it sucks." He gave me an even stare. "I could be more helpful if I weren't just sitting here."

"No, you couldn't." He brushed my lips with his.

Grey got out as a red truck pulled into the driveway. A man got out and stood, watching his approach. The two shook hands and walked toward the house, disappearing around the back.

The neighborhood was quiet, not a person in sight now that the dog-walker had moved on. I couldn't spot any action. Bored, I closed my eyes and must have dozed off. When I opened them, Grey was getting back in and the red truck was disappearing down the street.

"I wondered why the inspector was willing to meet; turns out he's a friend of Ender's," Grey informed me. "The propane tank exploded. Could've been the heat. He didn't see anything to indicate arson, and it's been deemed an accident."

"That's good news for the investor and Ender. Insurance will pay up and hopefully cut a check for enough money to rebuild."

I eyed the GPS after Grey programmed it with an address in another area that I was unfamiliar with. "Where are we going?"

"Surprise." He grinned at me, then shook his finger. "No eye-rolling."

He whizzed through the streets like he'd lived here his whole life. A couple of times, the GPS ramped up her snooty voice and told him to turn around, which he ignored. A few turns later, he turned onto a residential street. The properties were all colorfully painted, with fencing of one variety or another, and most had as many cars as they could squeeze into the driveway.

Grey coasted past a house the color of dried cat pee. A youngish man ran from the house, threw boxes into the bed of a pickup backed into the driveway, and ran back for more. Grey pulled down the block and U-turned, and as he did, a thug-mobile pulled up across from the pee house and opened fire, then roared off down the street after several seconds of shots fired.

Grey hit the gas and screeched up in front of

the house, jumping out and running over to the guy lying next to his truck door. He rolled over as Grey approached, so that was a good sign. Grey pulled out his phone, and the man jerked on his pantleg. A sedan squealed up and stopped, and two guys jumped out and ran up the drive. Yelling ensued between all the parties. I had the window down but couldn't make out the words. One ran inside and came out with two boxes, which he pitched into the trunk of the car, then jumped in and took off. The other man helped the guy to stand, threw his arm around him, and bundled his butt into the truck, then ran around to the driver's side and hit it in reverse.

"Is he okay?" I asked as Grey jumped behind the wheel. "And while we're at it, who is he?"

"Tyler Diggs." He shook his head, pure frustration on his face. "Grazed his arm. He was lucky." Unlike the other drivers, he drove sedately back to the corner, scanning the street as he went, then turned onto the busy highway. "I had my phone out to call the paramedics, but Tyler told me to mind my own business, with a few expletives, and to get out of there before I became a casualty."

"That was fast," I said, as red flashing lights and sirens breezed past us and turned onto the sleepy residential street.

Grey blew out an irritated sigh. "Tyler is a good example of why you don't do business with crooks and then renege on the deal. They get even, and it's never pretty."

"Surely the shooters weren't friends of Ender?"

"Nooo... Our young entrepreneur with the burned-out house got in over his head and borrowed more money than he could pay back. Used the property for collateral. His financiers found out that he'd already signed the property over to another party and didn't take it well. They issued a 'pay up or die' order."

"Those were the enforcers?" My tone let him know I was unimpressed with their skills. "Are they poor shots or was that just a warning, since typically you can't get money out of dead folks?"

Grey flashed me an 'are you done' look? He grabbed his phone and related what just went down to someone I assumed was Ender, adding, "Unless Tyler's stupider than he's already shown himself to be, you won't be seeing him around. He told me to tell you he's sorry. If he's got any sense, he's headed for another state." After a pause, he said, "No reason for a trip to the emergency room." He laughed, said, "Probably," and ended the call.

"Let's hope Tyler doesn't turn up dead in Georgia or somewhere," I said.

"You can bet that if he needs to see a doctor, one of his posse will have one on speed dial."

"Ender hired you to... turn Tyler's pockets inside out?" I asked, and the corners of his mouth turned up... much to his disgust, I was certain.

"I was there to tell him to stop ignoring Ender's calls." He eyed me with a stern glare, and I struggled not to laugh. "And since the fire was an accident, they would work out a new agreement."

"Is working for Ender going to be a full-time gig?" If I were him, I'd want to know more about the secretive side of Ender's business before working for him.

"I was just getting ready to share the news."

I shot him a squinty stare.

"Ender admitted that he didn't check Tyler out as carefully as he should have and some of the information he did get was out of date. He'd like me to do background checks on future clients." Grey maneuvered away from a driver who couldn't decide which lane he wanted to drive in. "He complained that he let several red flags get past him, that he'd been juggling too much and needs to delegate."

"I thought you wanted to restart your own business."

"That hasn't changed. He'd be my first client. He said that if it works out, he'll use me on other jobs when he hangs up his lawyer shingle. I like the idea of working for someone who knows my real identity, so I'm not a total fraud. And should anything go south, it would be good to have a lawyer handy."

"You two are getting to be fast friends."

"Told him not to feel obligated, just because he was a dick to me when we were growing up. He laughed and said I'd be a good fit for the job and he thinks we can work well together. In addition, he's offered to pass along my name to some associates that can throw work my way."

"You're going to need a social media presence, and I'm your girl." I looked out the window, trying to figure out where we were now. "Do you know where you're going?"

"Start practicing an apology, which I'll expect when I get us back to the condo."

"As long as we get there today and not sometime tomorrow."

Grey punched the gas. He headed back to the water and turned north on Highway One, then over to the Causeway, where he took the exit for Palm Island. He held out his hand. "I put that envelope of cash in your purse."

"I wouldn't give it back to the Old Coot." I bent down, fished the cash out, and handed it over.

Grey pulled up to the security gate and pushed the buzzer. "That's Kent's Mercedes, so he's home." He pointed to the car in the middle of the driveway.

He pushed the button again.

I kept my eyes glued to the windows, and there was no movement.

Grey tried again. He picked up his phone and

called, then left a message. "I was here as arranged to issue you a refund; you still want one, you can come get it." Grey backed out and headed home.

"I'm surprised the butler isn't in residence."

"The latest update I have is that Kent's got big problems. Millions were siphoned off, and yeah, he fingered his son, but he's also a suspect."

"How about some Mexican food and tequila shots? My treat."

"Not with a head injury."

"I have a bump on my head, and I'm not on meds. I've been good through this trying day of cops and robbers, and alcohol would hit the spot. That and a walk on the beach."

"I get it. You're 'tudey because you're hungry. To show off my amazing BF skills, we'll hop through the Bell and eat at home."

"Wait until I tell the owner of Cisco's that you dissed his five-star establishment for fast food."

"I'm calling your bluff."

"You're going to find out that I also know everyone and their brother, and when you've been here a little longer, you'll know the same people and their cousins."

Chapter Twenty

A week had gone by, and Grey's phone had only rung once. He was showing signs of going stir-crazy and dealt with his frustrations by running on the beach.

Avery had just left, after showing up with no treats and slapping down a rental agreement for the first floor of the office building with Hugo's name on it. I'd met him briefly and liked him; he made me laugh, and that sealed the deal. "Empty is not making you money, and you know how I feel about that," she said. Now the floors were all occupied, and Avery had taken over as building manager. Even though one wasn't needed, she was excited by the idea, and I let her make decisions, as long as she kept me informed. To be honest, I didn't want to do it.

Avery had negotiated a beneficial deal with Hugo, whom she liked. He got rent reduction in exchange for fix-it services, and if it wasn't in his bag of tricks, then he would recommend a non-shyster. She also pointed out that having his men around, who were built like tree trunks, was an added plus. She did have a talk with them about not crossing their burly arms and glaring at her clients. Winking at the ladies was perfectly acceptable.

Grey looked over the contract and was agreeable. He liked that two of the floors would be occupied, and that the men hanging around discouraged trouble.

He came out to my office on the balcony and set a sticky note on my keyboard. "I've decided that it's time to quit dragging my feet and get my life back, not just go through the motions. There's a murderer walking around that needs to be in jail." He sat down next to me.

Seven Donnelly. I recognized the name but waited for him to tell me how he wanted me to proceed.

"I want you to trot out your writer con and get a sit-down with my old partner. I'm certain he won't pass up the chance to talk to you, even if only for his own amusement. Depending on how it goes, I'll out myself—let him know I'm still alive and tell him he's a dick for not going to my funeral."

I thought about the so-called interview with Mr. Graham, and my cheeks burned.

"You don't have to worry about what to ask. I worked up a list of questions and emailed them to you. I'd like to know if anything new has turned up. Even though I'm 'dead,' I'm pretty sure he'd stay up on the case."

I typed the phone number in the search bar and clicked on the first result. "He's local."

Grey leaned in and looked at the screen. "I did some research and found out that Seven retired and moved down here to join the family business. He and his brother now compete to see who can sell the most yachts—big-ass ones. He wasn't difficult to locate, and I was happy to see that he'd made the move."

"I'll do it on one condition." I ignored his squinty-eyed stare. "Under no circumstances do you out yourself unless I give the thumbs up. One of my hidden talents is having a-hole radar, so I'll know if he's full of it or not."

"You like me." He grinned, thoroughly amused with himself.

"I'm a tad fond of you and don't want anything happening to you."

"Deal." Grey held out his pinkie. "Seven does have those hole tendencies that you're able to ferret out, but he's also a good guy. If he thinks you're available, he'll hit on you unless he's in a relationship."

"I'll wear a ring, and if that doesn't deter him, I'll whip out my phone and show him a picture of my six kids. I'll photoshop an extended hillbilly family in front of a barn, add in a goat and a couple of dogs for that downhome feel."

Grey barked out a laugh. "You're totally his type." He pulled his ringing phone out of his pocket and held it up so I could see the screen: Avery. He barely got out "hello" before she started talking. Whatever it was irked him and wiped the smile off his face. "I'll tell her and be right over." He hung up. "There was an attempted break-in at the offices. They couldn't get past the security doors but did crack the glass and jam the lock."

"Do I need to call the insurance company?"

"It doesn't sound like enough damage," he said over his shoulder as he walked inside.

I closed my laptop and followed him. "Hold up, I want to go. You leave me, and I'll follow you." He had his back to me, so I couldn't hear what he was grumbling. I trailed behind him into the bedroom and quickly changed into an A-line t-shirt dress and sandals, then grabbed my purse and left him to finish, taking up a post at the front door.

"You thought I was going to sneak out without you?" he said as he strode down the hall.

"You wouldn't do that." I didn't bother to hide my sarcasm.

Grey grabbed my hand and raced-walked to the elevator.

I grabbed my hand back and straightened. "I'd like to get to the car in one piece."

He chuckled as we rode down to the garage. After he unlocked the passenger door, he leaned in and bussed my cheek, followed by more laughter. He blew across town, maneuvering the one-way streets with ease, and pulled into the parking lot, taking his space under the tree. We got out and walked around the building, inspecting the side door and then the front; both appeared to have gone one-on-one with a crowbar-type instrument and won.

One of Hugo's men—I assumed, since he matched Avery's description—strolled up. He had a barely contained, neutral look on his face, the tightening of his shoulders and coiled muscles of his neck a dead giveaway to his mood as he approached. He turned his head and hawked out a mouthful of tobacco, not all of it landing in the street.

"Next time, get a little closer, so none of it lands in the parking lot." There's an eyeroll in my tone. "Better yet, get yourself a spitter thing."

"Spittoon," Grey whispered with a grin.

"Name's Floyd," he introduced himself with a toothy smile. "Sorry. Don't tell Mama; she'll kick my butt." He stuck his hand out to Grey, who took it.

Grey hooked his arm around me. "This is the owner, Harper Finn. I'm Steve, and my office is on the third floor."

"Nice to meet you." Floyd nodded at me. "Heard good things from Avery."

Speaking of the woman, the door flew open and she blew out. She waved to Floyd, who looked at her like she was a delectable morsel. "You're going to be happy with the upgrades I authorized."

"You remember the heads up you were going to give me before making any executive decisions?" I asked.

"I know that you're busy with your favorite client—me. Did you get the images I sent over to update my social media sites?"

"I've got my web designer working on it as we speak." I smirked at her, not telling her that the sites were getting an overhaul with an even splashier design. "Back to the upgrades that you authorized…"

"I promise, you're going to approve. I had security cameras installed. One at each entrance and one in my office, of course." Avery pulled her phone out of the pocket of her dress, scrolled through it, and thrust it at Grey. "Got a great picture of the wannabe intruder."

Grey took a long look and growled. "What the hell was he doing here?" He handed me the phone.

I stared at the screen. "That Rally guy. He's a long way from Orlando." I handed it back to Avery.

"Text Hugo his picture," Grey told Avery, who nodded. "Anyone sees Rally on the property, call the cops."

"If you want, one of the guys can sleep here the next couple of nights, in case the little butthead comes back." Floyd hung his head over Avery's shoulder.

"We'll talk," Grey said.

"What do you suppose he wanted?" I asked. "Quite the coincidence, him showing up here of all places. How did he get the address?"

"The only time you met Rally was when he intruded on your meeting with Jeff Graham," Grey mused. I nodded. "As I recall, Graham didn't introduce you."

"If I had Rally's phone number—" I eyed Avery. "—I could call and ask him. Since he wouldn't be expecting the call, he'd be caught off guard. It would be interesting to see what kind of explanation he comes up with for attempted breaking and entering."

"Give him a choice," Avery said. "He talks to you or you call the cops and press charges. Let him know you'll also be suing for property damage."

Floyd grinned approvingly at her.

"After you met, Rally disappeared inside the coffee shop. That must have been a ruse," Grey said. "The only way I can think that he could have gotten this address is if he ran the license tag on my SUV. It's registered here. The only thing that is, actually."

"Since he couldn't know you were the driver, he has to be looking for me," I said.

"Agreed. But why?" Grey grouched.

"What was his name again?" Avery whipped out her phone.

"Rally Charles," Grey told her. "He lives in Vista Isle with his parents, or did at the time of the investigation."

"Mr. Graham mentioned that he was a

neighbor, so I don't think he's moved out of the mansion," I said.

"You get an address, and I'll rearrange his teeth." Floyd cracked the knuckles on his meaty hand.

I looked down and winced.

"I'll go see what I can find out." Avery raced back inside the building.

Grey turned me to face him. "You're not to call Rally unless I'm sitting right by your side. Under no circumstances do you arrange to meet him without my bodyguarding services."

"Your old man here can't make it for some reason, I volunteer." Floyd was back to cracking his knuckles.

I nudged Grey with raised brows, grinning at the thought of him being Grey's stand-in 'old man,' but Grey was only in the mood to glare at that point. "Didn't your mom tell you that will give you big hands?" I said to Floyd.

He threw his head back and laughed, holding up two skillet-sized palms. "You can see I wasn't much of a listener."

A two-seater Jeep—a model that hadn't been manufactured in years, sanded and primed, with flecks of red still showing—rumbled into the driveway and parked. A twelve-year-old jumped out from behind the wheel and waved. The tie with a t-shirt was an interesting look, and his glasses hung over by a foot on each side of his face. I knew without asking that he was a friend of Avery's, although I didn't know she had children for friends. And law-breaking ones at that.

"Who are you?" Grey grouched.

The kid jumped back and stared, wide-eyed. "Dixon." His hands shot in the air. "I work here. Just ask Avery English."

"Relax," I told the kid, but it was also meant for Grey. I linked my arm in his and tugged.

"Sorry." Grey introduced everyone. "There's just a lot going on around here."

Dixon nodded and entered the offices.

"If you're ever hiring," Floyd said to Grey, "I'd like to take a stab at the job."

Grey fished his phone out of his pocket and handed it to the man. "Call yourself so I know how to get ahold of you."

Floyd handed it back with a big smile on his face. "You won't be sorry." Someone yelled his name from inside, and he waved and disappeared through the door.

Chapter Twenty-One

After having a short conversation with Avery, we headed home, and by the time we hit the parking garage, she'd texted me Rally's cell number. Grey grabbed cold drinks while I retrieved a burner phone, and we met out on the balcony. I sat down next to him and made the call. Voicemail. Again and again.

"How about I leave him a message: 'Answer or I'm calling the cops?'"

"So much for the friendly approach." Grey laughed. "Might as well. He probably thinks you're a spam caller and has no intention of answering, as least not without some motivation."

"I'm going to issue multiple threats." I grinned manically. "First to pick up the damn phone, and follow it up with a time and place to meet in person. To which I'll be taking my significant other—Floyd."

It was clear that Grey liked the idea but was hesitant. "Floyd's going to start asking questions."

"Maybe not. He hasn't so far. If he's lived in

Florida a while, he figures what you don't know... and if trouble comes back around and gets in his face, he can kick its butt down the block."

"My instincts are leaning toward Floyd being a good choice. I'm going to hit him with a few questions—ascertain his trustworthiness and make sure he can handle the job."

I picked up the phone, called Rally, prepared for voicemail, and left a message. "Rally, Brenda here. You tried to break into my building. You've got two hours to call back or I'm calling the cops."

"He knows that if you're calling, he screwed up, and he won't want the cops involved. He'd have to run to Daddy for bail money, and I guess he'd want to keep that from happening." Grey checked his watch. "If you don't hear back, then follow through and call the cops."

"He's going to call. On the off-chance he doesn't, I'll give the cops a copy of the security tape, and he can explain to them. Press charges, see how he likes that."

"I heard you cross-examining Avery on the Dixon kid. Does he at least have a learner's permit?"

"I object." I slapped my hand on the armrest. "During our friendly conversation, Avery told me that Dixon graduates from college in a few months and, in the meantime, earns college credit working for her." I made a so-there face.

"They met at a math symposium; it's where smart peeps go and lord it over each other about whose IQ is higher." I laughed, knowing Grey didn't believe me.

The burner rang.

Grey picked it up, checked the screen, and handed it to me. "What do you know, your threat worked."

"How are you today, Mr. Rally?" I asked in a saccharine tone.

"I didn't catch your name," Rally said in a snooty tone.

"Then you need to go back and listen to the message. After that, how about we meet for coffee and you can explain why you tried to break in to my office building?"

There was a long pause. "Ten o'clock tomorrow work for you?" The snootiness was gone.

"I'll text you the address."

"It would be more convenient to meet at your office."

If I had my way, he'd never set foot on the property again. "I'll text you the address of the coffee house. See you at ten." I disconnected.

Grey, who'd been scrolling through his phone, held it up so I could see the screen. "We'll meet here. I don't want him anywhere near Biscayne Bay."

I turned up my nose at the location he chose, which was on a busy highway in Miami, but agreed with his logic and texted Rally the address.

Grey got on his phone. "Got a job for you, if you can square it with Hugo. Don't want you to hack him off." He laughed at the response. He shot a few questions at Floyd, then hired him to bodyguard me, making arrangements to pick him up at the office in the morning.

"I take it Hugo's okay with you poaching one of his employees for the day?" I was happy to have oversized muscle at my side. Who knew what Rally Charles was capable of now that he'd been caught committing a crime?

"Floyd already told Hugo that he'd hit me up for a job, and everything's copasetic. If Ender's not full of himself and starts sending work my way, I'll start using Floyd when needed. If he's after a PI license, then I can set it up so he can put in the hours and get a legit license."

"That would be swell of you, sweetness." I frowned. "I'm going to miss you when you start hanging at the office."

"You're reneging on partnering with me?" He teased, amusement in his eyes.

"Oh no, I'm in… with one little caveat. I get right of refusal on the jobs and no hard feelings."

"Been thinking… there's no reason you can't take your laptop to the office. There's plenty of space to spread out. There's no beach, so I thought I'd hang up a wall-sized poster, add wave sounds for background ambience."

"That's sweet of you."

"Another perk: office hours won't be the crack of dawn until noon, like you're doing now."

"Sounds like a perk for you." I laughed. "As your partner, and in the spirit of full disclosure…" I ignored his suspicious stare. "I'm going to call your ex-partner and see if he'll consent to an interview."

"Seven's going to be full of questions. Do like you do me—answer with another question. Dance him around in that charming way of yours. That kind of nonsense will intrigue him, and he'll be eager to meet you, though he won't let on."

I faux glared at him.

Grey laughed me off. "Exaggerate. Let him believe you've interviewed everybody and then some, but don't give him a single hint as to what the others said. He won't be able to help himself and will want to know what you found out. And when he finds out you're full of it… too late. Pay for the coffee; that will assuage his ego some." Grey was thoroughly amused with his idea.

"And at some point, you're going to pop up and say, 'Look who's back from the dead'?"

"That's where my plan gets vague. I'm going to wait and see how your interview with Seven goes. If I want my life back, I'm going to have to trust someone in order to get anywhere with trying to track the real murderer."

"Do you think there's a link between the real

killer and the person that wants you dead?" I asked, having overthought the question a lot of late.

Grey nodded. "Or they're one and the same."

I picked up my phone. "No time like the present."

"Seven's going to ask how you got his number, and you're going to say…?"

"The truth, of course." 'Duh' in my tone. "His cousin's third wife." Grey laughed. "Or do you think I should be vague and, if he presses, say, 'Google search'?" I pulled the ex-detective's number out of my pocket. "I've already decided that if he doesn't answer, I won't leave a 'call or else' message." I crossed my lips with my finger. "I'm going with my Brenda persona."

"Yes, Miss Jones." Grey saluted.

I steadied my hand as I punched in the number and took a last-minute deep breath.

"Charm him, and you'll be fine," Grey whispered.

"Seven," he answered.

"This is Brenda Jones…" I launched into my writer spiel. "I have a few questions about the death of Mindy Graham that the others I've interviewed weren't able to answer, and I was hoping that we could meet and you'd clear up a few issues."

"How did you get this number?"

"411," I said with certainty.

Grey lowered his head, and I knew he was

laughing. I attempted to kick him, but he intercepted my foot and pushed it away.

"Who knew anyone still used that service." The smirk in his tone was loud and clear. "If you're going to lie about something, maybe do some research."

"I'm sorry," I said, not sounding the least bit. "I meant Google."

Seven actually laughed. "How many people have you interviewed for this project? How about tossing out a name or two?"

"Dozens," I said airily and attempted to steer the conversation to another subject. "I thought we could meet for coffee and a pastry. My treat, of course."

"Back to my question, which you ignored. Names?"

"It wouldn't be professional for me to disclose that." I sucked in a breath to steady my nerves.

"You're lucky that I have a flexible schedule… and then there's my curiosity. How about we make it lunch? You pay, and I'm in." Seven chuckled. "In addition, I'll be wanting a mention in this book of yours *and* a signed copy."

"How about: 'Without the input of Seven Donnelly, this book wouldn't have catapulted me to the bestseller list'?"

"Tomorrow at one? I'll text you the address, and we're agreed that this is a one-time deal."

I agreed. "I appreciate you taking the time to talk with me."

"Don't be late." Seven hung up.

"He went easier on you than I thought he would." Grey chuckled. "I'm wagering he chooses his favorite restaurant, an Italian hole in the wall that has amazing food and charges for it."

"The only time I grumble about price is when the food's terrible." My cell dinged, and I showed the screen to Grey.

"That's the place." He nodded at the screen. "I'm jealous. You need to bring me something to-go."

"You can eat it fresh from the oven if you come and sit at a table close by."

"Maybe, but I'd need sunglasses and a hat, and both would need to conceal my face. I'm trying to remember the layout. I say we get there early and pick an out-of-the-way table." Grey stood. "I've got a box to go through that's got some fun stuff in it. I'm going to mic you up for tomorrow. I have earpieces—flesh-colored, so they blend in with your skin tone—that make eavesdropping easier." He'd cleaned out the storage unit and moved the few boxes he had, which were currently stacked in the second bedroom.

Chapter Twenty-Two

The next morning, Grey woke early and was out of bed at the same time as me. I made the coffee while he picked out a dress for me to wear and affixed a mic under the collar. Grey tested it several times, and it worked loud and clear.

As we got ready to leave, he wrapped his arms around me and gave me a crushing hug. "You've got this. Anything goes awry, you've got me and Floyd as backup. Neither of us will take our eyes off that turd, Rally." He took my hand, and we walked to the elevator.

I took a breath to calm my nerves, but it wasn't working. Grey kept up an endless stream of chatter on the drive to the office, which was unusual for him. I appreciated him trying to keep my mind off the morning ahead.

"You don't have to worry about what Floyd knows or doesn't. I had a long conversation with him last night, and I trusted him enough to tell him what's going on. If I made the wrong decision, I'll only regret it if it comes back on you."

He pulled into the parking lot.

I leaned across the console and gave him a quick kiss.

Floyd — a carbon-copy of Grey in jeans and a dress shirt, and cutting a menacing figure — was leaning against the bumper of a truck. When he caught sight of us, he waved and climbed in the back of the SUV.

"Keep your eyes on Rally," Grey said. "I'm not expecting any trouble, but we don't know why he tried to break in or what he was hoping to find. The only priority is keeping Harper safe." He went on to explain what he expected. "You'll be introduced as Harper's boyfriend." No comment to that one. "If the little pissant puts up a fuss about you sitting at the same table, too damn bad."

"Don't you worry. I'll keep my eyes peeled, and Rally won't get any closer to Harper than across the table," Floyd said gruffly.

"I'll be interested in your observations," Grey said to Floyd as he pulled into the strip mall where the coffee house was located and cruised past the entrance. "Damn." He hit the steering wheel. "Rally's already here, sitting under one of the big umbrellas."

Floyd turned and stared.

"I'm going to park, and you two get out. I'll stay behind for a few minutes, and when I'm certain his attention is on the two of you, I'll circle around and grab a table."

Rally's attention went from scanning the

parking lot to his phone, which he picked up, then turned away and started to talk.

Floyd and I got out.

Floyd joined me as we crossed the parking lot. He moved with surprising agility considering his size. "Don't worry. Rally tries anything, and I'll rip his head off. There's a trash can at the entrance."

I laughed. "In case Grey forgot to tell you, my name is Brenda Jones." I caught Floyd's eyeroll and almost laughed again. "Another thing— don't be surprised by anything I say. I'll be making it up as I go."

"Gotcha. You say whatever you want and I'll go with it."

Floyd and I walked up the steps, cut across the patio, and sat opposite Rally Charles. He hung up without a good-bye, eyed Floyd, and straightened in his seat.

Out of the corner of my eye, I was relieved to see that Grey had claimed a table off to one side and out of Rally's view, unless he turned completely around.

Rally stuck out his hand. I ignored it. Anger flashed in his eyes. "Who's he?" He inclined his head toward Floyd.

"Her boyfriend. I wouldn't stick your stubby fingers in her face again. I'd hate to break them off." Floyd's tone said he wouldn't mind at all, and he followed it up with a hair-raising smile.

"What was so important that you attempted to

pry open both doors of my office building?" I asked.

"I could've sworn I heard someone yelling for help, and I couldn't turn my back," Rally said in an innocent tone. "Then it was silent, and I thought maybe I was mistaken. But I couldn't turn my back if someone needed aid."

I wanted to applaud his performance. I did give him credit for making eye contact while attempting to sell his lie. "That's your story?" Dumbass. "It needs work. I'm surprised you couldn't work up a better explanation, since you've had a couple of days to come up with one."

Rally's jaw clenched, and his eyes darkened. It was clear that he wasn't used to having his word questioned.

"How did you just happen to find yourself at my office building?" I asked.

"A fluke," he said with a strained smile. "Saw you on the road a couple of days ago and followed you, not realizing I was running late for an appointment. I made a note to go back later, hoping to catch you."

Yeah, sure. "We're here now. What did you want to talk to me about?"

"I overheard your conversation with Mr. Graham about writing a book about his daughter's murder. I'm the one you should interview, since we were friends. Although the ending will suck, since the murderer is dead and was never brought to justice." Rally's eyes gleamed, suggesting he thought justice had been served anyway.

"The problem with your theory that Grey Walker was the real murderer is that there was zero evidence." I struggled to keep the bite out of my tone. "I'm certain had there been any, he would've been charged."

"Mindy's body was found on his property. How else would she get there?" *Duh* in Rally's tone. "Since you want to talk evidence, there weren't any signs of her being dumped." He stared intensely. "Don't tell me that you're going with some theory of Walker's innocence. That will be a boring story, and anyone who knows the facts will think you were bought off." His lips curled smugly. "You'd change your tune if you interviewed a couple of the women he dated. Not a nice guy. In fact, a few of them reported that he had an explosive temper."

There had only been one woman mentioned in the articles I'd read, and I'd love to sit down with her. "You're volunteering to sit for an interview and answer questions so I can get the *real* facts?"

"You've not been overly friendly. What's in it for me?" Rally leered.

Floyd slid his chair closer to me, and the man pinned him with a glare.

"What I meant was that I'm one of the few people that could give you the real story of how everything played out." Rally leaned back in his chair. "You probably know that Mindy and I had been friends since childhood. We met in the second grade, kindred spirits. As we got older, we didn't spend as much time together as we wanted. It seems like I'm the only one who cares that Walker was never brought to justice. Just because he's dead doesn't mean it's too late to get the real story out." He flashed a secretive smile, letting me know he was the man with all the answers. "No one else is going to talk to you. I'm surprised that Mr. Graham agreed to meet with you at all, since a book is the last thing he wants."

"Do you have proof that Walker was the murderer?" I asked.

"I don't need to make anything up." Rally huffed. "Facts speak for themselves."

If he had the proof, why not go to the cops? I suspected he was full of himself, but that didn't explain what game he was playing. I glanced at Floyd, who was staring Rally down with a fierce expression. He fidgeted in his chair and looked around the patio, keeping his eyes averted.

"If I agree to this interview, you'd be willing to disclose all this proof you say you have?"

"You don't have to take my word for it. Once we've had the opportunity to talk facts, you can interview the rest of the players in the case. I can give you a list, since I know them all," Rally boasted.

I'd thought he was full of it from the moment

we sat down but that didn't stop me from wanting to hear him out, waste of time or not. "What do you expect in return?"

"Not money," Rally said, amused by the idea. "I'd want it in writing that I'd be listed as a co-author, my name the same size as yours on the cover. The upside for you is that my name alone would make it a bestseller."

Floyd snorted, which garnered a glare from Rally, who looked quickly looked away.

"In exchange, you'd be willing to answer all my questions and be available for any follow-ups?"

"I have a lot to offer to this project. Besides sharing my intimate knowledge, I also volunteer to accompany you on other interviews. Your boyfriend won't have to take any more time off work." He looked down his nose at Floyd, who bent forward, and Rally popped back in his chair, almost tipping over.

"Where my girl goes, you'll be seeing my mug." Floyd patted my shoulder with his meaty palm.

I winked and leaned into Floyd, which garnered another glare from Rally. I had no doubt that with Floyd as my bodyguard, nothing would happen to me.

Rally regained his composure and straightened up in the chair. "I'm certain that we can come to amicable terms. I'd also need assurance that your threat to call the cops is off the table, now that you know my attempted entry was purely innocent. Not to mention my showing good faith by meeting with you today."

His smarmy smile had me shifting farther away from him, even though there wasn't room to go anywhere. "You did show up," I said noncommittally.

"I'm staying at the W South Beach," he relayed in a snooty tone. "Once you have our contract drawn up and ready for me to sign, we can meet in one of the rooms, where we'll have plenty of privacy."

Floyd slapped his hand down on the table, and Rally's cup teetered. "There will be no meeting at a hotel. There's a coffee house on every corner, public library, don't care, as long as there's plenty of people around."

"Don't you trust your girlfriend?"

Floyd hunched up out of his seat. "You little…" he growled, and the smirk disappeared off Rally's face.

I grabbed Floyd's arm… part of it anyway. "Hon, I promise I won't go anywhere that there aren't a lot of people." I felt his muscles relax slightly and turned to Rally. "Before I sign off on you being a co-author, you'll need to give me something that shows it would be worth partnering with you. Show that you can produce, and to that end, how about setting up a meeting with Cathy Silver? Shouldn't be too hard, since you're friends."

Rally took his phone out and made a call. "Went to voicemail," he said to me, then said into the phone, "Cathy, I'm giving Brenda Jones your number; she's the one I told you was researching Mindy's murder." He hung up and sent a text. "I just texted you her number. I can also arrange for you to interview Mindy's sisters." Rally's offer shocked me, and it must have shown because he added, "They'd talk to you if I was the one asking."

"I wouldn't want to upset them by asking questions that make them relive losing their sister." I inwardly winced at Mr. Graham's reaction. If he could hear this pompous jerk, he'd have a flipping fit. "I'd rather not involve Mindy's family, but I'd be interested in the names of any other people you think might be helpful."

"If you're worried Mr. Graham would find out, we could keep it secret."

"I understand you are neighbors? You must have a good relationship with the Graham family." I already knew the answer but was curious what he'd say. "After speaking with Mr. Graham, I could tell his pain wasn't far from the surface."

"Our families are tight. We spend a lot of time together. I spend as much time with Mindy's sisters as I can; it's what she would've wanted, and it helps lessens my pain. They remind me of Mindy—free-spirited, loving. Even though I have my own business, I make time as often as possible."

I hated the idea of meeting the sisters on the sly. "Why don't we wait and see if we think their input will be needed?"

Rally nodded, clearly not happy. "Mindy deserves to have the story of her death truthfully told. She'd expect me to step up and do what I had to do to make sure that happened now that justice can't be served in her case."

"You mentioned your business—what is it you do?"

"I'm an investment advisor." Rally preened. "You need advice on money, I'm your man."

Not a chance in hell. I reinforced the benign smile I'd pasted on. Rally was certainly full of himself, and I'd had enough of him and needed a breath of fresh air away from him. I checked my watch. "I'm happy that we decided to meet," I lied. I needed a shower from sitting in this humidity, sucking heat, and had no time before meeting Seven. "We have to be going." I stood. "I promised that I wouldn't make my hon late for his appointment." I nudged Floyd, whose smile would've made my hair stand on end if I were just meeting him. Now it was reassuring.

"I didn't catch your name," Rally said to Floyd. "What is it you do?"

"None of your business, dude," Floyd grumped. "Your business is with my little petunia here."

I bit back a laugh. Petunia!

"I also have an appointment." Rally stood. "Call me when you have the paperwork. Don't take too long."

"I'll get my lawyer on it, but it won't happen overnight." Actually ever. I'd drag my feet with one excuse or another. Ditching him wouldn't be easy, so I'd better come up with something good.

"Don't get cold feet. It's the best deal you're going to get." Rally trotted off, leaving his coffee cup, even though the trash can was a foot away.

With a shake of his head, Grey followed Rally at a discreet distance.

"He's a lying goat," Floyd said. "If one thing that came out of his mouth was truthful, I'd be surprised."

Chapter Twenty-Three

Floyd and I walked back to the SUV, and on the way, I handed him the keys. He kept one eye on Rally as he slid behind the wheel. "What now?" I asked, since Grey was nowhere in sight.

"We sit tight and see what Rally does next. I bet it's frustrating him that we haven't pulled out so he can follow us."

A couple of minutes later, Rally drove past us in a Lexus, slowing to honk and wave.

"He's so full of himself," Floyd growled.

Rally drove to the exit and got in line to turn. As the cars stacked up, we lost sight of him. Grey showed up, and took over the driver's seat while Floyd got in the back.

"Rally may be interested in a book deal, but that's not all he's up to," Grey said as he slid behind the wheel. "I followed him to the Lexus, which is a rental according to the sticker on the bumper, then zigzagged back through the parking lot to make sure he didn't catch sight of me."

"He creeps me out." Note to self: check with Avery to see if she ran a background check, since it was something she liked to do. If not, get one.

"He spent the time hinting at what he had to offer and boasting of his connections. He did call Cathy, and it will be interesting to see if that pans out."

"I wouldn't trust him for a hot second," Floyd growled.

I nodded. "What bugs me is his lame explanation for showing up at the office and attempting to break in. I think he'd like to see his name on the cover of a book, but he's got another agenda."

"He just happened to see you out somewhere? Yeah, sure." Grey snorted. "We need to be careful."

"I agree with Grey. Rally's got an agenda, and you need to figure out what it is. If you need someone to rearrange his face, I'm your man." Floyd grinned. "Also, be careful. Rally's interested in you. He gets you off to himself, then what? If he came knocking for one of my sisters, I'd kick his butt clean off the porch."

Grey turned and gave me a fierce stare. "You promise me right now that you'll never go off and meet Rally anywhere. No matter what carrot he dangles." He glanced at the dashboard clock. "We might as well head to the restaurant; you can bet Seven will be early." He turned south and headed to the Coconut Grove area, where we were meeting.

"We didn't book Floyd," I reminded him.

"He's in. When I talked to him last night, I

went over the basics of what you're up to and these two meetings."

"I object to your wording." Both men laughed. I turned in my seat. "Very happy that you were by my side today. I had no doubts about my safety. By myself, I would've been totally creeped out."

"Anytime you need a bodyguard, give me a call. Don't be worried about me blabbing your business." Floyd held out his hand. "Give me your phone, and I'll plug in my number."

I handed it over the seat. "You can bet that Mr. Graham doesn't know about the friendship between Rally and his daughters. I wouldn't want to get them in trouble, but he deserves a heads up that the man is sniffing around. Graham made it clear that he had zero use for Rally."

"My guess is that it's all BS, like most of what he said," Grey said.

We rode in silence for several miles. After a while, Grey started questioning Floyd about his personal life, and we learned he was in his thirties, a local boy born and bred, and had a passel of family members nearby who were a close bunch. "Anything else would incur the wrath of my mother," he relayed with dread in his voice.

Grey then asked about his interest in becoming a PI.

"It took a while, but I passed the test for my

license. Now I need to put the hours in under someone else's license," Floyd said. "Hugo knows I'm ready to move on and this is what I'd like to do. He's a great guy and is willing to be flexible with my schedule, as long as I can give him a heads up when I'll be needed elsewhere."

Grey explained the type of on-the-job experience he'd need to get his license and what would be required. "Give me a couple of days, and I'll have the names of a couple people you can contact to get the training and hours you need. I have no doubt you'll be an asset to any company. I'm happy to use you when I can, but right now, I'm in the process of rebuilding and don't have enough to keep you busy full-time."

"I can be available whenever you need me."

"I've got the promise of a couple of clients, but so far, nothing's materialized. When it does, I'll be happy to throw work your way."

Grey turned on Bayshore and into the parking lot of Roma's, a charming brick restaurant across from the bay. He pointed to another black SUV. "What did I tell you? Seven's early." He parked off to the side of the entrance. "I'm going to wait this one out in the car." He tapped his ear, then picked up my phone and called himself, handing it back to me.

Floyd and I got out and walked into the restaurant. The lunch crowd was leaving and there were a few empty tables, so Seven was easy to spot at a corner table by himself. The picture

I'd seen online didn't do him justice. We walked over to the table. "Mr. Donnelly?" I asked.

The forty-something, blond-haired, blue-eyed hottie stood, towering over us. He belonged in the almost-seven-foot club. "Seven," he corrected, eying Floyd.

Floyd stuck his hand out. "I'm the boyfriend bodyguard."

Seven didn't seem surprised when he didn't offer up a name.

The waiter showed and took our drink order, all of us ordering iced tea.

In order to cut through the awkwardness, I contributed to it by saying. "I want to offer my condolences on the death of your partner."

Seven grunted. "Odd circumstances, since Grey never did drugs."

I nodded sympathetically in the ensuing silence. "As you already know, I'm investigating the murder of Mindy Graham for a book I'm writing. Anything you could tell me…" I launched into my prepared pitch. The man clearly wasn't impressed, judging by his stare.

He reached into a briefcase that sat on the floor, pulled out an iPad, and handed it to me.

"That's really nice of you, but I already have one." I didn't brush it away, but I also didn't take it from him.

"What I'd like you to do is pull up a website, something you've written, or your social media profile to prove that you are who you say you are." Seven's smirk seemed permanently affixed to his lips.

Damn. Of all the people who should've had that covered... I could've created a fake profile in an hour or two. I struggled not to show my frustration with myself and let his hand hang out there.

He set down the iPad and shoved it across the table. "Any time you're ready."

"I didn't want to divulge up front that I'm a first-time writer. I decided to put off creating those sites until I get a publisher. Currently, I'm in the research phase."

"Surely you have a personal social media profile, Facebook... something."

Now I knew what the deer in the headlights must be feeling. Caught.

"I can vouch for my petunia." Floyd slapped his paw over mine. "No one has ever questioned my word." And if they did, they got the moly beat out of them was left unsaid.

Seven eyed the two of us. "You know what I think?" he drawled.

Not really. I wasn't prepared to be called out and humiliated. My cheeks flamed. "I don't want you to think I'm wasting your time."

"Not thinking that." He squinted at me.

"You'd be my third interview. My first was Jeff Graham, and I just finished up with Rally Charles. A quick call to them would verify my story." He might call my bluff, but I couldn't actually see him doing it.

Seven's eyes narrowed. "Rally's here in Miami?" I nodded. "He have anything interesting to contribute?"

"Just that he was friends with all the players. He wanted to work a deal for co-authorship in exchange for his helpfulness."

Seven snorted. "Here's a tidbit that will pay for the cost of my expensive lunch: Rally can't deliver squat. Just because his father is a millionaire several times over doesn't mean that anyone's going to talk to his spawn. He's got some nerve."

"I could test your theory and have him set up a meeting with you."

"You do that. If he somehow manages to get in touch with me, I'd agree just to see what he had to say. You can be assured that the meet-and-greet would be turned back on him. Cops didn't get to question him as thoroughly as they would've liked, since he lawyered up. I'd be interested to hear what he has to say after all this time. I doubt he's got the brass ones to call."

Floyd laughed. "It would be fun to watch."

"Brenda Jones, is it?" Seven asked, disbelief in his tone. "You're going to have to show me something that proves you are who you say you are if you expect me to… What are you really up to?"

"The reason I called is simple—I'm after information about Mindy Graham. I'm sure it's hard for you to leave your detective training behind and take this at face value, but that's the truth." I thought that sounded good, but Seven didn't, judging by the fact that his eyebrows rose a foot. "You're kind of young to ditch the force. Bet that's a good story."

"None of your business. I took my awards and left with glowing recommendations. Against my better judgment, you've got five minutes. You're lucky I don't have it in me to pass up a free lunch at my favorite restaurant—the cost wouldn't pay for my time, but we'll call it even." Seven waved over the waiter, who passed out menus. "Everything here is excellent, so no matter what you choose, you can't go wrong."

My stomach revolted at the mention of food, slowing only slightly from the roller coaster ride it was on before once again kicking into high gear. "What can you tell me about Grey Walker's involvement in the case?"

"Zero. Despite what you read online, no one that knew him thought he did it. Who tried to frame him? That's still an open question. Surprisingly, the murderer covered their tracks pretty well, and those with ties to the case weren't forthcoming. I felt bad for Mindy; seemed like no one wanted the truth to come out. My guess is they feared it would uncover more skeletons."

I did my best not to flinch under his relentless stare and maintain eye contact. "Why did

Detective Walker resign?"

"The firestorm of publicity didn't show any signs of dying down. I sat him down several times and told him to be patient and give it time. But it's hard to ignore it when you're the one in the spotlight. The chief believed in him and still has the Graham file on his desk. He'd like to solve that case before he retires."

"Anything new?"

Floyd clapped his hand over mine and gave it a squeeze.

Seven glanced over, amused. "My best advice..." His smirk returned. "If you do uncover any new information that would be helpful in solving the case, turn it over to the cops and let them handle it. Getting your butt kicked is painful and can be deadly. Although I don't suppose your bodyguard would let you do anything too stupid." Noting my grimace, he added, "If you don't feel comfortable calling the cops, you can call me."

I'd had enough. I had a couple of personal questions but lacked the nerve to ask... not sure why it kicked in now.

The server reappeared at the table, ready to take our order.

I glanced at my watch. "My five minutes are up. If I learn anything of interest, I'll call." I reached in my purse and grabbed some cash, handing it to the server. "This should cover his lunch and a tip." I stood and nodded towards

Seven. "The rest is yours."

Both the server and Seven looked surprised. The latter nodded but didn't say anything to me.

Seven reached in his pocket and handed Floyd a business card. "If you're ever looking for a more challenging bodyguard job, give me a call. I've got contacts, and they're always looking for someone."

"Thank you for your time," I said.

Floyd hooked his arm in mine and propelled me out of the restaurant. "Just keep breathing. You can pass out when we get outside, though I wish you wouldn't."

"That was… Seven knows I'm full of it. I'm surprised he didn't boot me to the curb."

Floyd opened the car door. I slid inside, and he got in the back.

Grey leaned over and gave me a quick kiss. "He liked you."

I started laughing, releasing all my anxiety.

Chapter Twenty-Four

It had been a couple of days since my so-called interview with Seven, and Grey had been giving serious thought to outing himself to his friend. I told him, after he encouraged Floyd to accept whatever jobs Seven had to offer, that it was only a matter of time before he mentioned Grey in passing, and then what?

We were enjoying morning coffee on the balcony. Grey rarely went to the office, as we both enjoyed sitting outside and working. He'd gotten a couple of background check jobs from Ender, which he turned around quickly.

My burner rang, and I glanced at the screen, holding it up for Grey to see. Seven. Wonder what he wanted.

"Hello, Officer," I said when I answered, hitting the speaker button.

He snorted. "Did you talk to Cathy Silver?"

"I'm fine, and you?"

Grey grinned.

Apparently not seeing the humor, Seven remained silent.

"Okay then," I continued, not wanting to see who'd give in first, which would be me. "Left a couple of messages and didn't get a return call. After that, it felt stalkerish, and I stopped."

Grey scribbled a message: *Set up another meeting.* I nodded.

"I've got an unsettling update. About the time we were meeting, Cathy's car was found in the parking lot of an Orlando park. Her cellphone, keys, and purse, containing her ID and money, were on the floor on the driver's side. No sign of her."

"How long has she been missing?" These kinds of stories rarely ended well.

"Good question. Seems Cathy's estranged from her family, who had no clue. They hadn't spoken to her in a couple of months. Portrayed her as a difficult child that never grew out of it," Seven relayed with disgust.

Ouch. "I hope she's found soon and is okay."

"Since you owe me for the meeting—and whatever it was you were really up to—I'd like you to call Rally and see what he knows. If law enforcement calls him directly, he'll lawyer up."

"Happy to, since you're providing me with the perfect stall against his incessant nagging about the book contract. He's been burning up my phone." Which I'd ignored. "Now I can remind him that he hasn't upheld his end of the agreement, since Cathy hasn't called." This latest development should buy me a few more days before I begged off completely. "I'm giving you a heads up that I'm going to ask him to arrange a meeting with you. Since he knows everyone, you should be easy."

Seven's growling laugh was unsettling. "Good luck to that little dick trying to deliver on that one."

"Speaking of owing one another..." That was definitely a stretch, but what the heck. "I don't feel like I got my money's worth on that expensive lunch." I almost laughed at his snort and instead said, "Not through any fault of yours, of course. I'd like to set up another meeting."

"Not necessary. Just spit out whatever's on your mind, and it'll save both of our time and your money."

"I was thinking we could change it up; this time, I'll buy you coffee."

Seven laughed. "I get it. You're hot for me. Just say so."

Grey lowered his head and laughed.

"Not that you're not... anyway..." Grey's shoulders shook, and I kicked him. "Grant me one more meeting, and if it's a time-sucker, I'll lose your number."

"You get with your pal Rally, suck all the information you can out of him, and get back to me. By then, I'll have checked my schedule and know if I can fit you in."

I was never so happy to be hung up on.

"That's a yes to meeting." Grey continued to laugh. "It'll bug the heck out of him, wondering what you want. Especially since he doesn't have you figured out from your last meeting."

"I'm happy that I could be a source of amusement for you today."

Grey pulled me close for a quick kiss. "Get Rally on the phone and see what he knows or can find out about Cathy Silver. Time for him to live up to his end of the contract he's not going to get."

I flinched at the thought of telling him that, knowing he wouldn't go away with a quick wave.

"I don't recall any link between Rally and Cathy. Nothing about the two of them being friends came up at the time," Grey said. "Mindy didn't have many friends, and Cathy was the only one to come forward after her death. She shone in the spotlight for a short period and then disappeared."

"Isn't it bad news that her personal belongings were found and not her?" I asked. "I suppose there's some hope that she wandered off on her own and will turn up. Do these kinds of cases have happy endings?"

"A small percentage, and those usually turn up within twenty-four hours," Grey said, shaking his head. "You can bet the cops checked all the security cameras in the area to see if they yielded any clues."

"It's sad that no one close to her knew that she's maybe missing. Sounds like they had to be told by the cops."

"Unfortunately, people disappear all the time and no one knows until a body is found. You find out no one's seen them in years and there was no one to care." Grey handed me the burner. "Call eager Rally and find out what he knows about Cathy, if anything. I wouldn't divulge what you know; instead, fish around. Even if he knows nothing, you can use it to your advantage by getting Seven to show for coffee. Dangle details of the conversation, and he'll meet with you." He was amused by the idea.

"Expecting straight answers out of Rally is a stretch, based on our first meeting." I reached over and grabbed a file off the top of my stack. "Rally's background check came back." I handed him the folder. "Squeaky clean. Top credit score. Couldn't find anything about the company he bragged about. Not sure how new clients find him."

Grey glanced at the report. "This just validates what we already know — that he lives off his trust fund — and not much else."

I called Rally, reluctance a lead ball in my stomach. Leading him to believe that there was going to be a working relationship between the two of us wouldn't end well when he found out it had all been a con.

Upon answering, he skipped the pleasantries and asked in a superior tone, "You got a contract for me to sign?"

"You haven't delivered on your end. Cathy's not returning my calls."

"That's odd. I've never had a problem with her returning mine."

"I was there when you left a message. You're telling me she called back and agreed to call me?" If that was the case, I'd like to know when that happened.

"Now that you mention it… I'm such a busy man, it's hard to remember who I've talked to."

Grey and I looked at each other and rolled our eyes, then smirked.

Too bad he couldn't see us; it would prick his overinflated view of himself. "You could stop by her house and ask her to call. In the meantime, could you set up a meeting with Seven Donnelly? Since you're friends with the ex-cop, I'm thinking that you paving the way would make the process go faster."

After a pause, Rally said, "Donnelly's not the easiest man to get along with, but I'll see what I can do."

"Anything that you can do to facilitate my interviewing either of them would be helpful." The last person he'd want to contact was Seven, knowing the grilling he would get, ex-cop or not. I hoped he'd produce Cathy, because that would mean nothing bad had happened to her.

"I'll get back to you." Rally hung up.

"I'd be happy to never hear from him again. And ecstatic when this game is over," I said.

"Sorry to break it to you, hon, but Rally will call even if he has to make something up. He's salivating over that co-author title."

"When I shut him down altogether, he's not going to be happy." I shuddered at the thought of any kind of showdown and decided I'd definitely do it over the phone. I was very thankful he didn't know where I lived and would make sure it stayed that way.

"I appreciate everything you're doing. Once I bring Seven in, you'll be able to stop with all the subterfuge. I know it's grating on you."

"Have you figured out how you're going to break the news to him?" I asked. "I wouldn't blame him if he hangs up when I call him back and try to con him with what might turn out to be nothing."

"If he balks, promise proof of your identity." Grey laughed. "That will be a curiosity-tempter, since he thinks you're a fraud but cute. He spotted your crazy flag immediately and was attracted."

"You two are the crazy ones."

"Once the shock and anger wear off, Seven will be fine. Best of all, we can trust him." Grey stood. His wink had me on alert. "I've got a job. I was told I should fit in, so I need to change into tropical attire." He strutted to the hallway.

I whistled, which failed to stop him, and opted to yell, "Hold up. What happened to the spirit of upfrontness?"

"That's not a word," he yelled back and laughed.

I heard the bedroom door close. "He has to know everything. Why can't I have the same rule?" I mumbled to myself. I stood, picked up my laptop, and went inside. Grey's keys on the entry table caught my attention. I grabbed them and, on the way down the hall, decided on my own tropical look.

Chapter Twenty-Five

While Grey was changing, I threw on a multi-colored cap-sleeved dress; one look in the mirror told me I'd nailed "tropical." I hustled down the hallway, one eye out for Grey to reappear.

He briefly glanced up as he continued to eye every surface. "You see my keys?"

"They're on the dresser in the bedroom."

"I could've sworn I looked there." He stormed past me.

Knowing I had a small window to make my escape, I ran to grab my purse, fished his keys out of my pocket, and shot out the door. I was indulging in six-year-old humor, but what did I care; I was having fun. I rode down in the elevator and strode past my SUV, which had been returned by the dealership looking good as new. I hit the fob for Grey's SUV, climbed in, and locked the door. I didn't time it but knew it wouldn't take long for the hardened detective to trail me. I adjusted the side mirror so I could watch his approach and not be caught off guard and get the wits scared out of me.

My vigilance paid off when he approached and attempted to open the door. He knocked on the window, and I smiled up at him.

"Open the damn door," he roared.

I cracked the window. "Can I help you?"

"You set me up. I'm going to strangle you."

I made a face. "That plan of yours doesn't work for me."

He stomped around and knocked on the driver's window.

I cracked it and said, "I'll need your word that you won't dump me beside the road somewhere."

"Maybe." His attempt at an icy glare fell short.

I unlocked the doors. Grey slid behind the wheel and, without a word, backed up and drove out to the street. "I can't believe you," he hissed.

"Really? This is me we're talking about. I'm happy to remind you that the same can be said for you. You thought you'd waltz out of the house without a word, your smirk telegraphing that you were up to something, and planned to get away with it?"

He turned away without a word.

We weren't doing the silent thing. "Where are we going?"

"I'll let the client tell you. I can't believe you. As soon as I walked into the bedroom and saw no keys, I knew I'd been set up. Then you were gone. You won't pull that trick a second time." He shot me a side-eye.

"I'll just have to up my game."

He tried to hide his smile, but wasn't quick

enough, and it had me smiling too. He grasped my hand in his. I leaned back as he zipped through the streets and it became clear where we were headed.

I retrieved my hand and pulled out my phone. "Why are you calling Grey without one word to me about what's going on?"

Gram cackled into the phone, and I pulled it away from my ear. "Who's the detective? You or him?"

"You know damn well I can be nosey when the need arises."

"Language, young lady. You weren't brought up on the porch."

"I apologize if I caused a setback to your sensibilities," I said, not bothering to hide my sarcasm.

"You know full well I don't have any of those." Gram's cackle had my brow bunching and me jerking the phone away from my ear again. "Did he ditch your behind? If not, when are you going to come knockin' so I can have the iced tea ready?"

"You and I both know you always have a full pitcher in the fridge. So cool your heels until we get there. We're halfway, but he drives like an old woman, so it'll be a few."

"Hey," Gram squealed. "Present company excluded. Got to go; there's the door." She blew kisses through the phone.

"You're so rude," Grey faux grouched. "It

surprised me, when I got your background check back, that you had a blemish-free record. Not even a traffic violation." He laughed, enjoying the faces I was making at him. "Since you checked me out, thought I'd do the same."

"I suppose you're disappointed that the report wasn't full of salacious activities, arrests, a trip or two to jail?"

"I got what I wanted, a boring read."

"What does Gram want?" I demanded. "Besides to ogle you. She and I are going to have a talk. She needs to keep her drooling to herself."

Grey laughed. "One of her neighbors has been robbed several times."

"Anyone else?"

He shook his head. "She wants me to apprehend the culprit before word spreads around the complex and everyone gets freaked out."

Grey pulled into the retirement village, and the guard waved him through.

I turned in my seat. "He's supposed to ask your name and, if you're not on the list, call Gram, not just let you in."

"Except that I have a sticker." He waved to the corner of the window.

"When did Gram send you one of those?"

"I peeled yours off." He shot me a toothy grin.

"And you have the nerve to complain about *my* outrageousness." I shook my head. "When I showed up and couldn't get in, then what?"

"I have faith that you'd come up with something." He continued to grin as he pulled into Gram's driveway.

"I no longer feel bad about jacking your keys."

"You felt bad?" He clearly didn't believe me. "So sweet." He leaned over the console and brushed my lips with his. "Try to behave."

I rolled my eyes.

Gram had the door open before we got out. I walked up and pecked her on the cheek, giving her a big hug.

"I thought you two were going to sit in the car all day and smooch it up," she said with a growly laugh.

"I'd have been game."

"That's my girl." Gram patted me on the back, then turned and enveloped Grey in a hug. "Send me the bill for your services; Ruby Stellar is on a tight budget." She socked him in the arm, and he scooped her off her feet and into a hug, then set her down when she squealed. "Come on in, and I'll get Ruby's skinny butt over here to tell you what's going on. According to my crime shows, it's better to get the deets from the victim."

I linked my arm in Gram's and led her into the house. "Have a seat and tell Grey whatever, and I'll play hostess." I ushered her to a seat at the same time someone knocked on the door. "I'll get it." I opened the door to a woman with bright red hair frizzed outward, an untidy mess. "Ruby?" She nodded, a smile igniting her face, and I stepped back.

"That would be me. We haven't met, but I've heard a lot about you." The woman clapped me on the shoulder.

I stumbled back a step and caught myself. "Knowing Gram, there's a little bit of truth and a whole lot of bragging."

Ruby laughed and slid past me, waving to Gram as she crossed the room and plopped down next to her.

I went into the kitchen as Gram introduced Ruby and was happy to see that she had a tray set up, so all I had to do was add the pitcher, and I wouldn't miss a word. I walked back into the living room, tray in hand. Grey stood and took it from me, setting it on the coffee table.

"I don't know how they're getting in," Ruby told Grey. "The first time, only cash was stolen, and they seemed to know right where it was. The house wasn't turned upside down or anything. The next time, jewelry went missing, and two days ago, a few pieces of silver."

"If you wouldn't mind giving me a tour of your place? That way, I can get an idea of the layout and give you a recommendation or two to tighten up your security. Don't worry, we'll get this figured out." Grey smiled reassuringly.

"I had one of those doorbell camera things installed, but it never worked right." Ruby sighed with exasperation. "Even had my grandson check it out. He did his best but couldn't get it working either."

Grey stood and extended his hand to Ruby, and the two left.

I filled a glass with tea and handed it to Gram.

"What's up with you and cutie patootie?" Gram asked.

"I like him. We just seem to get along. Have ever since we met."

"I haven't heard yet how you two met." Gram rubbed her hands in anticipation.

I never lied to my Gram and wasn't going to start now. "Can I ask a huge favor? Can we hold off on this discussion?" Gram's brows went up, and I added, "You're going to have to take my word for it that he's a great guy."

"This has your craziness written all over it." Gram stood and enveloped me in a hug.

"Why do I always get the blame?"

"Because you take after your Gram." She laughed and sat back down.

"What's the story with Ms. Ruby, whose hair color almost matches her name?" I asked.

Gram fluffed up the ends of her hair. "Ruby thought I'd look good with a rainbow of color." I groaned. "Don't worry, I told her she was off her rocker."

"Gram, really? You could've been… well, nicer."

"You can't live in this joint and have thin skin. You do, and you'll be in a snit all the time."

"Joint?" I shook my head at her. "The owners

of this upscale establishment would take exception to your description."

"As long as no one gets hurt and the cops don't show up..." Gram snorted. "If they were that picky, they'd have made mental health testing mandatory, and then half of us wouldn't be here."

"They might have a mass exodus if the residents find out someone is robbing the *joint*."

"Don't you think it's weird that she's been the only target?" Gram asked in a conspiratorial tone, as though we weren't the only two in the house. "We need to get this figured out and stopped pronto."

"What *we* need to do is let Grey handle it." I barely refrained from wagging my finger at her. "That's why you called him in the first place. Nice of you, by the way, even though you trampled my feelings, not being your first call."

"You needed to press your hand to your forehead." Gram demonstrated. "Unleash a long sigh." Another demonstration. "Sauce it up a bit."

Instead, I unleashed an exaggerated eye roll that made her laugh.

"What do you hear from your old man?" Gram asked.

"Not squat." I regularly searched online for any mention of his name. I knew if I found one, it wouldn't be good. Avery was also keeping an eye on his bank accounts, and he hadn't been dipping into them. "When he returns," I said firmly, refusing to have it any other way, "I plan on repeating your 'old man' reference. That's after I'm done yelling and laying down a few rules." I'd probably envelop him in a hug and not let go. "There will be no more damn disappearing acts. Or else."

"You'll send him to his room and throw away the key?" Gram hooted.

"I've got one better. I'll cry."

"That would be mean of you. But it's sure to make him crumble. Remember the time Skippy teased you until you cried? Your *old man* came out of the house and caught him in the act, grabbed him by the back of his shirt, and shook him until he slipped his arms out of the sleeves and ran. The chase was on." She smacked her knee. "Little turd just barely got in the house and locked the door."

"What I remember was that Skippy told anyone at school who'd listen that my dad was dangerous and to stay away or risk bodily harm." I glanced at the clock on the mantle. "If those two aren't back in three minutes, we're going to go hunt them down. We should've gone along so we could eavesdrop."

"I've heard the story over and over. Told her to file with insurance, but that would've required a police report and she's dragging her feet about doing that. She waits too long, and insurance will deny her claim. That's where lover boy comes in—I'm hoping he'll talk some sense into her." Gram flicked her finger at the pitcher, which I deciphered as *fill up my glass*.

Finally, Grey and Ruby came tromping back through the door.

"I got the security camera reconnected and it's in the process of uploading the footage it stored. Whoever hooked it up didn't know what they were doing," Grey said. "I've got the code to access the history, which I'll go through tonight. In the meantime, I've instructed Ruby, and now you, not to discuss the break-ins with anyone. Wouldn't want word to get back to the culprit."

Gram zipped her lips. "I know how to keep my trap shut."

"I'll get back to you tomorrow, once I've reviewed everything." Grey held out his hand to me, and I stood. "I'm headed back to the office to get started, so you'll have peace of mind."

I stood and hugged Gram, then waved to Ruby. "Nice to meet you."

Grey felt in his pockets, not once but twice, and leveled a stink eye at me. "I'll need my keys."

Gram giggled, knowing what I'd done.

"Here they are." I pulled them out of my pocket.

Grey hugged Gram, and whatever he whispered in her ear, she laughed, then winked at me. He hooked his arm around me as we walked out.

When the door closed, I asked, "What did you say that had Gram laughing?"

"I told her that I was going to kill you."

Chapter Twenty-Six

On the drive home, my burner rang, and I groaned as I fished it out of my purse. The number on the screen was 'unknown.' "I wonder who this is." I answered with, "This is Brenda," then pushed the speaker button.

"Cathy Silver. Rally told me you were trying to get ahold of me." Her voice was all babydoll breathy.

I glanced at the screen again. "I had a different number for you."

"Once I decided to get a new phone, I went with a new number and threw the old phone out."

"I'm happy to hear from you, since I saw a report that you were missing," I said.

"That was a misunderstanding."

"I don't know what Rally told you—"

Cathy cut me off. "That you were writing a book about my friend Mindy Graham. I don't know why he didn't tell you that I don't like talking about the murder. It's upsetting and creepy that I knew someone who was murdered."

"I hoped that we could meet up and talk in person."

"No, no, that's not possible." She mumbled to herself, and I held the phone closer, trying to figure out a word or two. "Ever since I filed a police report about that horrible detective, I've been inundated with interview requests. I find it all bothersome. If you want one quote, here it is: I'm not sad about what happened to the man."

I reached out and patted Grey's arm. "I'm sorry that I won't get to meet you." I didn't know what else to say.

"The only reason I called is because Rally's been such a sweetheart to me, and I just couldn't find it in me to say no. I want to be helpful, but I just can't. I don't want to do anything to hurt his and my friendship. I'd appreciate it if you told him that I was fully cooperative. It's not like he'll ever know that I wasn't unless you rat me out." She giggled again.

"I understand. I appreciate your calling."

"Don't forget, not a word." She let out a long "ssh" before hanging up.

"That giggle of hers made her sound unhinged," Grey said. "I had about a hundred questions, starting with whether the cops know that she's not missing after all."

"I agree that there was something off about her." I hadn't been paying attention to the drive and was surprised to see we were home, Grey turning into the garage. "Even though I asked,

I'm fine with not meeting with her. Not sure what I'm supposed to say if Rally asks how our conversation went, though."

"My skepticism speaking… I think Rally knew Cathy wasn't going to be the least bit helpful, but being upfront doesn't get him his author gig, hence the lie."

"I'm ready to shelve this project. I'm tired of insinuating myself into people's lives to ask questions that they have no interest in answering. Once was sort of fun… until it wasn't. I'm over it, and telling Rally to buzz the hell off is long overdue." I squeezed my eyes shut for a second. "If you want to get the 'boyfriend of the year' award, you need to come up with one heck of a story for me."

"I'll tell him." Grey cracked his knuckles.

I pulled him to me and kissed him.

When we got back upstairs and through the door, I said, "I should let this drop, but I'm curious. Since the number Cathy called me on isn't the same as her old area code, I'm going to get Avery to trace it."

Grey and I went out to the balcony and worked on our respective laptops. I sent off an email to Avery while Grey scanned the security footage. It wasn't long before he came up with several images of a guy in the twenty-something range coming out of Ruby's house on the days she said items had gone missing. He didn't appear to be the least bit nervous about getting caught.

He turned his laptop around. "You know this guy?"

"Never seen him before, but Gram could probably ID him if he's a regular visitor in the neighborhood."

"I'll email her and attach the picture."

"Free tip: you need to do that in person. If you don't and she does recognize him, she'll drag Ruby along and the two will confront the guy. Worst case, one or the other goes by themselves. And telling them not to will blow straight through their ears." I attempted a wind noise, and it sucked. I laughed at myself.

"What about this motorcycle?" Grey pointed to the corner of the screen.

"It's not against the rules to drive one around there, but I haven't seen any of the residents riding one." I leaned in for a closer look. "For this guy to get past security, he's either got a sticker or is on someone's guest list, since he's shown up several times."

"That will make tracking him down easier. You can bet the guards at the gate will remember him and his motorcycle."

"You start asking them questions, won't they be compelled to call in the cops?" I asked. "And if you're able to ID the owner of the bike, then what? Isn't there a certain amount of risk if you confront the man? That could jump ugly quick."

"I'm thinking this is a good case for Floyd to get his feet wet. I'll take him along, show him the ropes, and whatever we turn up, I'll let him take credit for."

"You're putting a lot of trust in someone you barely know. I'm hoping he doesn't out you."

"Unless my instincts are totally off, I think he can be trusted. If not, you need to take a vacation."

"Then you're coming with me."

"Being Steve Smith was fun for about five minutes. I'm ready to get on with life, and to do that, I need to find out who wants me dead."

I couldn't stand the thought of anything bad happening.

"My only other option is to stay completely hidden and immerse myself in this new identity, which would require me to break the law, and that's not who I am."

My phone rang, and it was Avery. "The number was from a burner purchased in Ft. Lauderdale. The woman was local when she made the call."

"Does it ever scare you how good you are at this?" I asked.

"It's fun." Avery laughed. "As much as I enjoy running numbers, and I do, I love when I get one of your calls needing information."

"You're the best. I'm certain there will be more requests. Just know that you can tell me at any time that you've had enough and don't want to do it anymore."

"No chance of that happening." We both laughed and hung up.

Grey had gotten up and gone into the house to make a call of his own while I was talking and now came storming back outside. "I called Ruby to set up a time to see her tomorrow, and she had people over. I couldn't very well interrogate her about who, and it took everything in me not to throw questions at her, especially since she was telling her guests that the security agent on the phone was the one who fixed the system and was now reviewing the tape."

"It was too exciting for her to keep to herself." I wasn't surprised in the least and should've have realized this would probably happen. "Did you lecture her ear off?"

"So close... Instead, I lied and told her that the footage didn't yield anything, hoping that she'd relay that information to her guests. She did after someone questioned the 'Oh damn' she muttered."

"How did you leave it?"

"I somehow managed to control my grumbly tone, reminding myself she was an older woman and this was probably too exciting a situation for her, despite it also having the potential to be a dangerous one. Told her that I'd see her in the morning to give the system one last check to make sure it's working."

"Be sure you give Ruby the stern look you

have on your face right now. She'll melt into a puddle."

"Why doesn't it work on you?"

I laughed.

Chapter Twenty-Seven

The next morning, Grey left early, but not before joking that he found his keys where he'd left them.

"If I didn't have client issues that require my immediate attention, I'd be hot on your heels." I waved him off, picked up my laptop, and went outside to join a scheduled online meeting.

It was almost noon before the door banged closed. "Want something to drink?" Grey yelled as he stomped toward the kitchen.

"Surprise me," I yelled back.

Grey took a shortcut, coming out the slider from the kitchen, and closed the distance between me and him, handing me a cold bottle of water. I winked at him.

"Turns out the thief is Ruby's grandson," Grey announced as he sat next to me. "I also found out that the little pecker has a drug problem."

"How did Ruby take it when you showed her the pictures?" I felt bad for her, knowing how glowingly she spoke about her family.

"She took one look and went off on a tirade, lecturing my ears off." Grey huffed. "Respect for the fact she could be my grandmother is the only thing that held me in check. Floyd stood by with a silly smirk, reading my mind. All I said in the car was 'payback,' and he laughed."

"Why was Ruby irked at you?"

"She apparently forgot that I didn't know the guy's identity and was mad that I didn't divulge it in the phone call. Could I get a word in? No. She stood right in front of me and started going on about some half-baked plan she was concocting to confront her grandson on her own."

"Did you take my advice to trot out the stern look and tell her that her idea sucked?" Judging by his evil glare, I guessed the answer was no.

"I wanted to leave her to her own bad ideas but couldn't, knowing that she could get hurt... worse than her feelings. That's when Gram showed. Having spied my arrival, she waltzed through the door and told Ruby, 'Shut up and listen.' It was like Gram had deflated her. She threw herself in a chair, arms crossed, and glared."

"Leave it to Gram to cut through the nonsense."

"Gram listened politely to Ruby's plan to confront the grandson, Kash, on her own."

"Kash, huh? Which he's short of." I laughed.

"That wasn't funny."

I made a face.

"Gram told her, 'Of all the stupidest. You need

to listen to a professional and not go off half-cocked. If you weren't going to listen, why have me call him?' I thought she went too far when she asked what kind of funeral Ruby wanted."

"Love Gram. She cuts through the BS—sometimes, anyway—and gets to the point."

"Ruby had wound down by this point and was out of fight. I offered to drive her to where her grandson was living so she could confront him with backup."

"I take it she was amenable?"

Grey nodded. I felt bad about laughing, so I covered my mouth. I got the stern stare, which I liked.

"While I had some cooperation going, I gave Floyd a signal, and we hustled both women into the car. Floyd, the ass-kisser, charmed Ruby and got her smiling, and even to laugh a couple of times. I told him later that he didn't have to rub it in. He told me that if I had a southern mom and mom-mom, I'd also have the skills to get back on their good side and fast if I knew what was good for me."

"I was going to suggest that for the next old peep case, you take Gram, but heck, you've got Floyd."

He turned and grinned at me. "Thankfully, it was a short drive. When we got there, the garage door was open, the motorcycle from the security footage parked inside. Kash was holding court with a couple of friends, and judging by the smell, they'd been smoking weed."

"With the garage door open? What a great way to irritate the neighbors into calling the cops."

"Gram stepped up and told his friends to hit the road. One started to tell her off, but Floyd cracked his knuckles." Grey laughed. "I bet they were finding out just how fast they could move."

"His hands are like skillets; they could knock you into the next life."

"Ruby got in Kash's face and confronted him with the pictures. He launched himself into her arms and pled for her understanding. That's when he confessed that he had a drug habit, aside from the weed — he likes to snort cocaine."

"Swell."

"Ruby wrangled a promise out of him to go to rehab and took his word that he would. Having been down this road during my cop days, I'd say chances of him following through are slim."

Kash would only go if forced, and that wouldn't work either.

"It was Floyd who stepped up and asked how he fenced the stuff. Pawn shop, apparently. Floyd then told Ruby that if she wanted the stuff back, to make sure Kash accompanied her, as she couldn't redeem the items on her own. She'd need his signature. At that point, Kash smirked. I walked out before I could wring his neck and left Floyd to tie up the loose ends."

"Don't be mad at yourself; it doesn't sound

like there was much else you could do."

"Kash stole from his grandmother, and when confronted, he ran a con that she sucked up, believing every word. Floyd told me on the drive back that he offered to change Ruby's locks, and she agreed. So he's picking up what he needs and going back."

"The ladies are going to be happy to have a new man to fawn over."

"I warned him not to turn his back on either woman or they'd jump him and want to go for a ride."

I laughed, despite knowing it was true. "Everything was amicable when you left?"

"Surprisingly. Seriously happy that I took Floyd. He had more patience than I did. When I had time to think about it, I realized that the last thing Ruby wanted to hear was that her grandson was the culprit. If given the choice, she'd rather not know and let it go... although she wasn't taking into consideration that he wouldn't have stopped until he cleaned her out."

"Gram will probably warn Ruby, but she needs to ban Kash from the village until he gets his act together. Word leaks out to the neighbors, and they'll turn on her." I smiled at him. "It was amazing of you to help Ruby gratis and do everything you've done, when I know you're paying Floyd."

Grey looked embarrassed. "More news. Ender called on the way home. Simon Kent was arrested at the airport, getting ready to board a flight to the Caribbean. He's been charged with felony embezzlement. He'd been having money troubles due to some bad investments and stole from the corporation. Wilson was in on the whole thing. Father/son con. Since the son is out of the country, he'll have to be extradited, which will take a while. Depending on his finances and whether he has access to cash, he can keep moving around and make it that much more difficult."

"Why hire you?" I snapped.

"It's Ender's theory that after Kent hung his son out to dry, he thought it would show his innocence or ignorance of what happened if he hired me to attempt to recover the money. Wilson was already out of the country, and Kent stupidly figured he was untouchable. Had he gotten an earlier start and not waited until everything was crumbling around him, it might've taken the spotlight off him, but not for long. When you're under pressure, that's when you start making a lot of mistakes."

"You're taking the case coming to an abrupt end rather well."

"Never liked Kent. Shouldn't have taken the case to begin with, but I got caught up in it being the first one as Steve. Can you imagine if Grey Walker had been involved with an embezzlement case?" He shuddered. "The pieces didn't fit, and from the first, I was wondering what Kent was trying to pull. I'm happy he didn't return my calls and I was out early on. If he was willing to let his kid take the fall, no telling what he'd do to a stranger."

Chapter Twenty-Eight

The next morning, Grey took his frustrations out to the beach. When I heard the door slam shut, I looked up and caught sight of him in workout clothes, sweaty and rumpled, as he headed to the shower. I went to the kitchen and made a fresh pot of coffee, then perused the shelves of the pantry and gave brief thought to going to the grocery store so I could at least pretend that I cooked. Dismissing the chances of that, I assembled a tray and took it out to the balcony. I hated to waste the view of the sky and water, which were the same perfect shade of blue today. Breathtakingly gorgeous.

Grey came out, coffee pot in hand, set it on the table, and sat next to me, leaning over to kiss my cheek. "What are you up to?"

"Just sit there and enjoy the breeze." I pressed down on his knee, turned my legs sideways, and tossed them over his lap. "Now you're trapped."

"I need to spend more time out here with my feet up, enjoying the view. Then I wouldn't be so grouchy."

"You're the easiest." I winked, which made

him laugh. "You've had a bulldozer run through your life, and you're still standing. Mark my words, you're going to come out better than ever."

"If I ever find out who hired you, I'm going to thank them and then break their face."

I laughed. "You have plans for the day, sweets?"

Grey made a face. "I know that look, *sweets*, and since you haven't answered my earlier question, which you promised to stop doing… today, huh?"

He hadn't extorted that promise out of me, but I wasn't about to remind him. I shook my head and pulled my burner phone out of my pocket. "You want to reconnect with Seven; I'm going to make that happen. If I can get the man to move his tuchus today, then I'm going for it." I called and pushed the speaker button. "I'll be happy when I can throw this phone in the trash."

"So soon?" Seven said when he answered.

"I'm hoping you're free today and I can buy you an overpriced cup of coffee."

"You're going to have to come up with something more than coffee."

"Talked to Cathy, and if you want to hear what she had to say, you'll need to meet with me. To add to your excitement about our get-together, I also got her new number, which you can pass along to one of your detective friends so they can close the missing persons case, if they haven't already."

"Or I can pass your name along to them, and they'll soon be pounding on your door. It's a crime to impede an ongoing investigation," Seven grouched.

"If I get a vote, it's no." I ignored his chuckle. Grey squeezed my free hand. "You wouldn't want to miss out on your big surprise, would you?"

Seven grunted. "Hate surprises."

"You and most people. If this particular one doesn't live up to your standards, I promise to go away and not blow up your phone in the future."

Dead silence.

Grey poked me.

"Five minutes of your time. But I suggest you block off more than that, or you'll wish you'd listened to me." More grunting on his end. I'd bet that he was arguing with himself about whether to blow me off or not. "Time and location, and I'll be there."

"The Bike Shop on Flagler in an hour. If you're late, I'm not waiting."

"You won't be sorry."

"Uh-huh." He hung up.

"That didn't go as badly as it sounded," Grey reassured me.

"I'm going to go change. I'm thinking early is better than cutting it close. I don't want to give him a reason to skip out on us."

* * *

The Bike Shop turned out to also be a coffee shop. In addition to meeting customers' caffeine needs, they offered bike repair and rental services. Seven was early. He'd commandeered a table on the patio and was leaning back in the chair, feet on the railing, surveying everything from behind his dark glasses.

I turned to Grey as he parked not far from the entrance. "You're coming with me?"

"I've been looking forward to this meeting. I'll be by your side—the silent, brooding type—and see how long it takes Seven to make me."

I cupped his chin in my hand. "You're certain Seven won't do anything crazy like arrest you?"

"Being presumed dead isn't a crime. And even if it were, he'd at least recommend a good lawyer."

We got out, and Grey held my hand as we crossed the parking lot. Seven had us in his sights the whole time.

"You've got five minutes," Seven said with a glance at his watch as we sat down. "You trade the galoot in for a punier model?" He nodded at Grey.

"Be nice," I admonished. "Would be a shame if he had to rearrange your face."

Grey snickered.

Seven gave me an even stare. "You going to introduce us?"

"Maybe later."

Seven snorted. "You talked to the elusive Cathy? Did she have a reason for letting people think she'd met an ugly end?"

"Now that was a weird phone call. She refused to answer any questions about anything, stating that she only called as a favor to Rally." I pulled a piece of paper out of my pocket and pushed it across the table. "That's the number of the burner she used. I also found out that it was purchased recently. Also noted is the address where it was bought."

Seven's eyebrows shot up. "Nice work, Brenda. It's still Brenda, isn't it?"

I ignored the question and his smirk. "Cathy's story about the old phone was that it stopped working and she got a new one, along with a new number. We both know that's a lie."

"Interesting." Seven looked at the paper and then at me. "Here's your freebie: I checked with my source, and the missing persons case is still active. He's very interested in this information, which I'll be passing along. If he's got more questions, do you mind if I give him your number? I also told him that Rally bragged about being friends with "all the players.""

"Isn't there some kind of anonymity for sources?" I managed not to roll my eyes. The last thing I wanted was to be involved in a police investigation.

"Where's my surprise?" Seven cocked his

head as though peeking under the table. "Can't be very big." He hadn't looked Grey's way since we sat down.

"We should have a rule—one asks a question and the other answers." That garnered a beady glare. Okay then. "I'll go first. Patience. I started this book project because I want to clear Grey's name and I needed your help to do it."

"What do you think you're going to uncover that the cops haven't?"

"If the situation were reversed, Grey would do it for you."

"He's dead," Seven said evenly.

"Except I'm not," Grey grouched.

Seven turned to him and scrutinized him closely. "You're telling me you're Grey Walker?" he asked skeptically. "Nice try, pal. He wouldn't go out in public looking like an overgrown bush, and I happen to know he owns a razor. That scraggle is... a mess." His lips quirked, just barely.

"Remember when Pixie—the love of your life, one of them anyway—dumped you, and you drowned your heartache in tequila? You claimed to have eaten the worm but couldn't remember where you bought the swill. I still think that part was BS. You ended up face down in the bushes all night, waking when the sprinklers came on." Grey went on to remind Seven of more of his life events that had ended in him commiserating with his friend, alcohol.

"Peggy," Seven barked. "You never could get her name right, which was a sex-killer when you said it in front of her. And even knowing that, you did it anyway."

"Give a guy a break. Couldn't help it—she dressed like one of Santa's elves, and the bootie shoes... I mean, dude..." Grey shook his head.

"When ole Pix was in the mood, she probably blew his socks off." I grinned at Seven and got the stink eye from him.

Seven kicked his chair back, he and Grey stood, and they hugged. "Where? What the hell?"

"It's a story you're not going to believe. Even I've had a hard time with it." The two men sat back down. "As Harper said, I'm hoping for some help to get my life back on track."

Seven's eyes followed Grey's as he smiled at me.

"Harper Finn. That would be me." I waved.

Seven scrutinized me closely. "I knew you were full of it."

"It's quite the story. I'll let Grey tell you."

Seven's face said, *Yeah right.* "You know who's going to be happy? Our old boss. He's still intent on finding Mindy Graham's murderer and clearing your name of any suspicion. He felt guilty about what happened to you, but he got caught up in a political firestorm."

"No hard feelings. On my last day, we spent a long time talking, and he wished me well."

"You're obviously not dead, so whose corpse was that?" Seven asked.

"Big misidentification. And when I heard about my demise, I decided not to correct the misunderstanding. I had a damn good reason. I'll start at the beginning."

I nudged him under the table. "I think there's a few things you could skip over."

Grey smirked at me.

"You two?" Seven scissored his fingers.

Grey laughed.

"What happened to your usual type—mousey, doesn't say much?"

I bit back a laugh.

"You must be in the coo-y, everything's fantastic stage. You're going to drive him crazy." Seven flashed me a knowing look.

"Harper saved my life," Grey said adamantly.

So there. I squinted at Seven.

"Can I get your word that everything I'm about to tell you stays between us until we agree that others need to know?" Grey asked.

"Anything you need."

"I was trudging along in my dreary life, major bad attitude and not doing much to turn it around, and then I met this hottie—" Grey waggled his brows at me. "—over coffee. Being a gentleman, I walked her to her car and—"

"You can skip forward in the story, don't you think?" I asked. "What happened right after that isn't really relevant."

"I disagree, sweets." Grey grinned. "It's integral to the story of how we met. Where was I?" He winked. "I don't remember anything after that until I woke up cuffed to her bed."

"Yeah, sure." Seven's laugh conveyed that he didn't believe that. "One look, and you're, 'I'll hook up with this one.'" He laughed again. "You have a sister?"

"If you like older women, my Gram would jump you in a hot second."

"It's a sweet story, but I know you too well, pal." Seven managed to stop laughing. "Can't wait to hear the rest."

Grey told him everything he knew about the contract on him, which was very little. It wiped the smile off Seven's face.

"What the hell, man?" he growled and turned to me. "You have no clue who hired you?"

"None, and not for lack of trying. I had the phone number traced, but it was shut down. Same for the bank account."

Seven turned his attention back to Grey. "If you hadn't gone off on your wounded high horse and stayed in touch, we could've partnered up and be making a go of it on our own."

"If we had, you could've ended up in the crossfire," Grey said. "Whoever was willing to shell out a million bucks to see me dead wouldn't have balked at a little collateral damage."

"You got a plan for how you're going to uncover this person's identity?" Seven asked.

"Everything so far has been a dead end, which is why Harper offered to interview people about the Mindy Graham case. That hasn't uncovered anything... except people that have no interest in bringing a killer to justice."

"There are a couple of officers we worked with that are retired and living down this way," Seven said. "I'm thinking we could pool resources. Get the chief involved, cover your backside, and make sure we don't cross any lines. We could start by getting you some 'I'm alive' publicity."

"The first thing the person who put a hit out on Grey is going to do when it hits the news is hire someone else," I snapped. "This time, they might find someone actually willing to do it."

"We'll get a good plan in place before doing anything," Seven said. "Did you commit any crimes while you were staying out of sight that would make you vulnerable?"

"Hi, I'm Steve Smith." Grey held out his hand. The two men laughed. "Other than the phony name, nothing."

Seven turned to me. "What about you?"

"I'll admit that my 'getting to know Grey' efforts were a little questionable." He didn't need to know anything else.

Grey grinned at me.

"Why do I think there's so much more to this story?" Seven asked.

"Because you're an ex-cop, and it's

instinctive," I answered, which quieted him for the moment, but I knew it would probably come up again.

The two men talked about what they'd been doing since their days on the force. Then bandied about ideas about how to proceed with getting Grey's life back, and who would've shelled out a cool million to see him dead. Mr. Graham seemed the logical choice, since it was his daughter that was dead. We all thought it had something to do with Mindy's death, as neither of them could think of any other reason that someone would be holding a grudge. The two went over past cases, and none stuck out as being likely to result in someone wanting to exact that kind of revenge.

Seven questioned me about my interviews, then said, "I'm eliminating Graham. He turned over the diary because he's friends with our old boss, and I don't think the chief would be able to overlook the kind of mental breakdown that would result in him thinking that hiring a hitman was a good idea."

"The chief told me about that on my last day."

"I still haven't heard from your pal Rally," Seven said to me. "Not that I expected to. Give him a call and tell him you were able to set up an interview through a friend of a friend's cousin and you'd like him to go along."

"That ought to make him squirm."

Seven told Grey that he'd clear his schedule and give him a call in the next day or two so they could come up with a plan of action.

Chapter Twenty-Nine

It had been a couple of days, and Grey and Seven had been burning up the phone, strategizing a plan for Grey to reclaim his life. They were getting together today, and Grey told Seven to meet him at the office building so he could show him around.

While they were doing that, I sat in the car and made a complete nuisance of myself—burning up Rally's phone, leaving more messages about today's upcoming interview with Seven, and making sure to tell him the time and location. I'd set up a meeting at the same coffee shop where we'd met Seven. Tired of the game, since I'd bet Rally had listened to everyone, I left one last message: *Cancelling meeting with Detective Donnelly. Will reschedule when you're available.* Seven and Grey had debated whether he'd show or not and decided on a definite maybe.

That got Rally's attention, as he called back immediately. "Sorry, I've been out of cell range due to a family emergency. Go ahead to the meeting without me, and I'll make it up to you."

Yeah, sure. He was a terrible liar. I'd wondered what his excuse would be, since he had no relationship with Seven and that would have been evident. Seven would have enjoyed calling him out on it. "If I have any questions after speaking with him, I'll get back to you."

Grey came back and slid behind the wheel. "Introduced Seven to Avery. He did a double take at the large eyeglasses that covered her face and, after a few traded barbs, called her a nutjob. I laughed and didn't tell him it was my special name for you."

Seven pulled out of the parking lot and disappeared from sight.

I punched Grey's arm. "Avery probably loved it."

"She told him he should take the stick out of his… but then called him a hot piece."

I laughed, sorry I missed it. I told him about my short conversation with Rally.

"If you're going to lie, don't tell one that's so easy to check out. My guess is that he didn't figure you'd get Seven to meet with you," Grey said, then shut off the engine and got back out. "I'm getting in the back."

I ran around and got behind the wheel. "Want to see how fast I can go?"

Grey groaned. "No, I do not."

I pulled into the parking lot of The Bike Shop, and Grey told me where to park, pointing out that Rally was only a few spaces away, having recognized his Lexus. I glanced over and saw Grey scrunched down in his seat.

"He's not going to be able to see you, is he?" I asked.

"With the window tint, he'd have to press his face to the glass. If he comes this way, I'll pull my hat down and pretend I'm asleep."

I got out and walked across the parking lot, acknowledging Seven and sitting down. We'd already agreed that this would be a short meeting so I could report back to Rally about how uncooperative the former officer had been.

Seven tapped his watch. "Five minutes for real this time."

"We could play a game of questions, make the time go faster."

He snorted. "Rally dude is a bit obsessed with you — showing up and spying from the parking lot. Time for you to boot him to the curb."

"I'm going to tell him I'm in over my head and tabling the project." I didn't look forward to that conversation. "What's your plan when I ditch you in about a minute?"

"I'm walking you to your car, then confronting Rally. I want to see if he's got any useful information or is just being a pain." He stood, downed what was left of his coffee, and tossed the cup into the trash. "Might as well be now."

We walked out to the parking lot and split up. I got in the SUV and waved. "Wonder how Rally's going to react to being caught?"

Grey looked out the window as I drove out. "He's probably not happy."

I glanced in the rearview mirror and saw Seven looming over the driver's side of Rally's car.

We were back at the condo when Grey's phone rang. It was a short conversation. "Seven and Rally went back inside for more caffeine. Rally sheepishly admitted to making stuff up so he could be part of your writing project."

"I thought he had too much ego for that," I said.

"He claimed to be insinuating himself into your research because he and Mindy were such good friends, and if it shed light on her case, all the better. Rally answered all Seven's questions, but it's anyone's guess whether the little worm was telling the truth."

"Maybe that's the last I'll hear from him." One could hope.

"He told Rally not to waste his time. Predicted the book project wouldn't get off the ground."

* * *

Grey and Seven had devised a plan, and Seven worked a deal with someone he thought was a friend to break the story, hoping to smoke out the killer. The reporter friend jumped the gun, however, and "Grey Walker alive and living in Miami" appeared the next day as a front-page item on an online gossip rag that people claimed not to read but devoured. At least the picture was an old one that didn't match his current appearance.

Seven called, livid, and updated Grey, who took the news in stride. His attitude was "it was coming out anyway," but he agreed that it would've been nice to have more control over when.

It didn't take long before the original burner rang. I'd been halfway expecting it but still jumped at the sound that broke through the quiet of the morning. I'd kept it charged in case the client who wanted Grey dead decided to get ahold of me.

"The story of Walker being alive better be fake news, or you're a dead man," the man practically spit through the phone.

"Fake news," I growled back, happy for the voice distortion app, which was still running. Grey had jumped up at the first ring and beat it back to the office, which he'd turned into an electronics headquarters. He was in the process of tracing the call; I just needed to do my part and keep the man talking. "In case you forgot, there's a death certificate on file."

"Stupid-ass drug overdose. That's not what I paid for," he barked.

"Dead's dead, and the overdose makes for far fewer questions. Or did you want the cops all over the case, hunting a cop-killer? It wouldn't matter that he wasn't still on the force."

"For a million bucks, I wanted a bullet between his eyes."

I could feel his anger vibrating through the phone. "Your bill still has an outstanding balance. Two million. And you didn't pay the full amount."

"You greedy son of a… you're lucky you're still alive. And trust me on this one—that could change any day now."

"Save your threats." I upped my game to match his strident tone. "I'll settle your bill by putting that bullet between *your* eyes."

The call terminated abruptly, which I was thankful for. The adrenalin rush from keeping up with the man started wearing off, giving me the jitters.

It took a while before Grey walked back out on the balcony, phone in hand. "Good job." He bent down and kissed my cheek. "The call was local—Miami Beach. The phone was purchased from a gas station down at the beach. How many could they possible sell?" he mumbled to himself, then answered, "Not many. I'm thinking that for a few bucks, we might get a look at the security tapes."

"I'd hit up the overnight guy," I said. "Terrible hours and probably not a lot of pay. Not to mention dangerous in some areas. Probably not down here though."

"I've got the GPS coordinates he was calling

from." Grey flashed his phone my way. "I'm going for a ride, check out the area. Don't worry." He waved off my unspoken objection. "I've no plans to get out of the car. Whoever called is probably long gone, but I want a look around. I'd invite you along, except I know you've got a conference call getting ready to start any minute. You are not to go outside." He finger-wagged. "Since you're not expecting anyone, do not answer the door. Your friends have keys. Not that I'm expecting any trouble; just being careful."

"You're going to call and reassure me that you're not out cruising the beach on foot, looking for a stranger who knows what you look like while you have no idea about him."

"I'll call and keep you updated."

I got the quickest kiss before he flew out the door.

I only half-listened to the business call, wondering every second what was happening with Grey and keeping one eye on the screen of my cell. Next time, and there'd be one, I'd go along, no matter what I had to reschedule.

I breathed a huge sigh of relief when Grey texted, "On my way home."

Chapter Thirty

The next day, Grey and Seven approached the guy at the convenience store, and when he heard "cash," he gave them access to the security tapes. Grey had taken a USB drive and downloaded everything, and they were going through them at Seven's.

I stayed home, busy with a few business issues of my own. Mid-morning my phone rang, Avery's face popping up on the screen. "What are you up to?"

Avery groaned. "Not good news. Another break-in. Funny thing—they attempted it during business hours, when they had every chance of being caught. My client had just left when the alarm went off. In case you wanted to know, it's loud. I asked the security installer to juice up the sound so it could be heard in the next state, and he delivered."

I hoped the neighboring businesses didn't get attitudinal and report us to the city for a noise violation. "Any damage?"

"A little to the door facing the street. I've got one of Hugo's men checking it out."

"I'll be right over." I stood and grabbed my laptop, piling my files on top. "On the way, I'll call Grey; he'll know what to do." We hung up.

I headed to the bedroom for a quick change into a skirt and top—casual without looking like I'd been sitting around the house, which I'd been doing—then grabbed my purse and flew out the door.

On the drive over, I called Grey, and it went to voicemail. I parked at the back of the parking lot and got out, going to meet Avery and a strange man, who led us around to the front.

"Dolbert, ma'am," he said with a crooked grin, then wiped his hand on his pants, sticking it out. "Don't you worry none; I can fix this right up."

While he flirted with Avery, I took a closer look and whipped out my phone for a couple of pictures. The 'Closed' sign must have seemed like an invitation to come in for a look around. The lock had been damaged, along with the padlock that held a chain wrapped around the wrought iron door. Not sure why Hugo thought that was a good idea, but looking at it now, I had to agree that it kept whoever it was out.

Avery sidled up beside me. Dolbert had disappeared. "I reviewed the security footage, and it was a lone person. They either knew where the cameras were located or got lucky. They kept their head averted, so we didn't get a clear shot of their face."

"I don't understand." We'd backed up and

were looking up at the building. "Who attempts a break-in in the middle of a weekday, with a truck parked out front? If they'd looked in the garage, they'd have seen your car. If I were a thief, I'd have my eye on your Porsche instead of a bunch of electronics."

"I was thinking maybe it was a young person who thought vandalism would be a fun way to blow the morning." Avery looped her arm around me. "The upside is you won't have to file a report with insurance."

"If whoever it is had gotten inside, I'd be calling the cops. Wish Grey would call."

"What are you thinking about so hard?" Avery asked.

"You'd think that being on a street that's out of the way would protect us from break-ins. Guess not."

Avery's phone rang, and she glanced at the screen. "I've got to take this; it's a client. Be right back. Don't go anywhere."

My phone rang, and it was Grey. I walked across the parking lot to the SUV and leaned against the side as I told him what happened.

"I'm on my way after I help Seven with a favor for the neighbor. He needs something moved into the house, and it's too heavy for him to carry by himself."

"I'll be waiting."

As I was putting my phone away, a young woman walked into the parking lot — dressed casually but expensively, long brown hair pulled up in a ponytail—and flashed me a friendly smile. She looked familiar... maybe. I couldn't place where I'd met her, or maybe it was just that she resembled someone I knew.

"Emily." She thrust out her hand.

"Harper."

She appeared surprised but smiled. "I work two buildings down. We had an attempted break-in, and I decided to check and see if anyone else had the same problem."

"Did they get in? You have damage?"

"They damaged the lock but didn't get in." Emily scanned the parking lot and then the building. "This is our first break-in. I never would've thought it would happen in this neighborhood; it seems so safe. You can't tell by looking, can you?"

"It was nice meeting you." I edged away, the woman's relentless stare had begun to unnerve me. "I need to get up to my office."

"Let me give you my card." Emily reached into the pocket of her dress and pulled out a gun, shoving it in my face. "Let's go up to your office together. I'd hate to shoot you, but one wrong move and you're dead."

"Do you know how to use that thing?" I froze, staring wide-eyed down the barrel.

"You want to find out?" Emily cocked it.

"What do you want? Money?"

Emily waved the gun. "Get moving."

I wanted to scream, but there wasn't anyone around. Her fierce glare told me that she wasn't bluffing about shooting me. "I need to take my keys out of my pocket."

"Slowly," she barked.

I pulled them out and opened the door, avoiding the elevator and heading to the stairwell. If I got the opportunity, I'd push her down the steps. I didn't stop until I got to the third floor, knowing there were Hugo's people on the first and Avery on the second. I didn't want to risk any of them getting hurt.

At the second floor, Emily complained, "How many more floors?"

"One more." I turned slightly, and she was several steps behind me. Giving up on the idea of knocking her down the stairs, I continued up to the third floor and opened the door, struggling to clear my head. I had one chance to knock that gun out of her hand and hope it didn't go off. And I'd need to catch her off-guard.

"This is your office?" Emily looked around, careful to stay back. "Sit in the chair." She waved the gun and, with her free hand, pulled a pair of handcuffs out of her pocket. "Catch." She tossed them at me. "Cuff your wrist to the armrest."

I knew it was now or dead.

"One wrong move," Emily clucked, as though she'd read my mind, "and you'll suffer. I need you alive—for the time being anyway—and it's your choice whether you want to be writhing in pain until the end, begging me to end your life."

I cuffed my wrist, but not securely.

Chapter Thirty-One

"Can you at least tell me what you want?" I asked. "This can't be personal, since I don't think we've even met."

"There are any number of ways of meeting." Emily twirled the gun around and blew on the muzzle. "This is a good one. Fun, don't you think?"

"I'm having a great time."

"Now, now. Sarcasm." Emily took out her phone and called someone. When they answered, she said, "Says her name is Harper." After a pause: "Same woman." She looked at me. "Brenda or Harper, which is it?"

What did she want with Brenda? I'd lie, but she apparently already knew we were one and the same. "My pseudonym."

Emily turned her back and lowered her voice so I couldn't make out what she was saying. I knew I hadn't interviewed this woman. I stared at her and finally remembered. It was the ear-grating giggle that gave her away. Cathy Silver. Mindy Graham's best friend. I vaguely recalled the one photo I had, and even though she was older, she didn't even remotely resemble the pic

I'd seen or the shy, reserved girl that Rally had described. Hearing only bits and pieces of her conversation, I realized she'd attempted to disguise her voice in our previous conversation.

When she hung up, I said, "You never did say why you're here." I hoped it wasn't to kill me, but it seemed to me that that was exactly what she had in mind.

"What were you thinking?" Cathy tsked. "Poking around in a case that had been finally been put to rest with the death of the cop. Oops, bad choice of words." She clapped her hand over her mouth. "The news of his demise showed that barely anyone was still interested in the story, since the coverage lasted about a minute."

Mindy's father. Her sisters.

"If you were thinking to make headlines with your stupid project, no way could that happen." Cathy waved the gun. "You got a phone on you?"

I reached across my body, pulled it out with my free hand, and held it up.

"Get Grey on the phone and tell him to get his butt over here."

Thinking quickly, I forced a confused expression onto my face. "Who? I don't know anyone named Grey."

"Grey. Grey Walker. The man you've been living with."

"What the hell are you talking about? His name's Steve."

"What's with you two and the phony baloney names? Not sure how you managed to hook up with a dead man. Or didn't you know?" She wrinkled her nose. "Call now and tell him to step on it. One word of warning and kaboom."

Wrong sound effect, but I didn't think she'd care one way or the other. "I don't know who you're talking about," I said, hoping that playing ignorant would buy some time I could use to my benefit.

"Yeah, sure. Have it your way." Cathy laughed. "Hilarious if you didn't have a clue as to your boyfriend's real identity. Whoever you think he is, get him the hell on the phone and over here before I lose my patience. This time when he dies, no one will notice."

I called, and when Grey answered, I said urgently, "Steve, there's an emergency at the office. There's been a plumbing leak. I think I got the water turned off, but not sure. Dad will have a fit when he comes in tomorrow and there's water everywhere." I hung up without giving him a chance to respond and kept my phone in my hand, knowing he'd call back. It was almost immediate. I pushed the button to block him, since that would put him on alert, then silenced it.

"Toss it on the floor." Apparently pleased with what she'd heard, Emily turned her attention back to checking out the office.

"When Steve gets here, then what?" I asked. "You kill us both? What did either of us do to you?"

"Steve." Cathy laughed again, clearly thinking it was hilarious, and threw herself down in the chair behind the desk.

How in the heck did I get into this situation? Rather than focusing on how soon I'd be sucking my last breath, I decided to try some negotiation. "We can make a deal." I attempted a smile and failed. "I'm sure we can come to a mutually beneficial agreement, one where you don't end up in prison for the rest of your life."

"Shut up," Cathy snapped. "You're getting on my nerves."

Mobster flashed into my mind. Who would take care of him, put up with his temperamental moods? Avery maybe. My thoughts went to my friend, who was one floor down. I hoped with everything in me that she wouldn't come up here wanting to talk.

While Cathy entertained herself on her phone, I tried to contain the sick feeling mounting in my stomach and rolled my cuffed wrist to the side of the armrest. Tears stung my eyes and blurred my vision. Using my free hand, I swept them from my face. I don't know how much time passed; I'd put a clock on the shopping list if I got out of here alive. I tugged gently on my wrist and realized I had some room to wiggle about. One hard yank and I could be free of it, but that would be a dead giveaway. I leaned back, continuing to work my arm, closed my eyes, and peered from under my lashes, keeping an eye on Cathy.

The door flew open and hit the wall, Grey filling the doorway. His eyes grazed past me and landed on Cathy, who pointed her gun at him. He stepped inside and closed the door. "I'm the one you want. I assume you're here to avenge your best friend's death."

"Avenge Mindy's death," she mused, as though it was the first time she'd thought about it. "Sounds good. No one would hold me responsible, since you're a killer who got away with murder." She laughed and waved him to a seat.

"Let her go." He nodded toward me, giving me a wink she couldn't see. "You might get away with killing me, but not her. The death of an innocent bystander would weaken any self-defense claim."

The door opened again, and Rally blew inside and looked around, a big grin on his face, surveying the room and waving a gun around. "Happy to see I didn't miss anything." He strode in and shut the door, crossed the room, and leaned against the corner of the desk, looking smug. "You going to kill them here?" he asked Cathy.

"Might as well. It would be too much work getting them downstairs, since I doubt they'd go willingly. They'll be found that much sooner, but it can't be helped."

"If this is retribution for Mindy Graham's death—" Grey eyed the two. "—I didn't kill her and don't know who did. You don't have to believe me, but you have to know that there wasn't any evidence against me. Hell, I barely knew Mindy; why would I kill her?"

"I thought finding Mindy's body on your property was all the evidence the cops would need," Cathy said. "If I had it to do over, I'd have followed through on my idea to plant a personal item of yours on her body or nearby. If I'd thought of it at the time, I'd have climbed one of your trees and gone in through a second-story window; no one ever locks them. I can climb better than any squirrel," she boasted.

"You killed her?" My mouth dropped open. "Didn't you grow up together?"

"It's her own fault. She was going to tell everyone... I had to stop her. My life would've been ruined. Not to mention that my fun would've been over," Cathy lamented.

"What have you got planned?" Rally asked.

"I'd just shoot them and be done with it, but there are other people in the building," Cathy told him. "I don't know how many, but you know that when they hear shots, they'll call the cops. I'm thinking shoot them anyway and be prepared to bolt out of here."

Since all eyes were on Grey, I tugged and

maneuvered my wrist, bunched up my fingers, and was finally free.

"You're so bloodthirsty." Rally laughed.

"Please… like anyone's going to miss him." Cathy turned her stare on Grey. "The public will think the 'He's alive,' article was a hoax. Besides, it garnered little interest anyway. Wonder what the gossip outfit paid for the tip?"

"Since it appears you two have made up your minds about killing us, at least tell us why," Grey said.

"Should I share?" Cathy asked Rally.

"Instead of a last meal, consider it a last conversation." He laughed.

You're hilarious.

Cathy unleashed a dramatic sigh. If she'd wanted all eyes on her, it worked. "Everyone always thought Mindy was a troubled person. Let's face it—anyone who knew her knew she didn't have the smarts to set you up for her murder."

"That's a bit harsh," said Rally, the lifelong friend.

"You have to agree that it was hard listening to her constant moaning about how misunderstood she was."

Rally turned his gun on Grey. "Don't think about moving. And don't bother denying that's what you were thinking; it's written all over your face."

Grey held his hands up and took a step back.

Cathy cleared her throat, clearly not happy that the attention had drifted away from her. "It was me," she said, ta-da in her tone. "Since I didn't have a rich daddy to cover my tracks, I had to use what I had, and that was dumb-ass Mindy."

"You killed her!" I still hadn't gotten past that part. If she hadn't been pointing a gun at me, I'd have slapped the eyeroll off her face.

"Of course, I killed her. It was fun and... I was the one to orchestrate every bit of trouble we got into and still managed to be an innocent party... well, maybe not every time. But I'd convinced her to stay quiet or it would be the end of our friendship." Cathy sounded disappointed. "But all good things must come to an end."

"Why leave her body on my property?" Grey grouched.

"It took Mindy two minutes to fall in love with you." Cathy shook her head; clearly, she didn't get it. "She was devastated when she figured out it was only going to be 'one perfect date.' She moaned on and on until I thought I'd barf. I thought she'd never give it up. As her bestie, I had to encourage her blather, no matter how irritating."

"So Mindy finally wised up that you were behind all her problems. Then what?" Grey prompted.

"She never understood why she got blamed for things she hadn't done. That's because when I decided to venture off on my own, like the time I robbed the neighbor's house, I always left evidence that she was the culprit. It was kind of fun to watch, wondering what her reaction would be as she finally put the pieces together. Her final mistake was getting in my face and threatening to tell anyone who would listen about all the havoc I created in her life. Boo-hoo."

Not a bit of remorse. I struggled not to show my contempt.

"I had to beg her for another damn day after promising to confess to her family and mine. Couldn't believe that she thought I'd do that. Then I had to figure a way to grab her attention and get her to cooperate, so I told her I had a surprise, which she didn't believe, but I had her hooked once I told her I'd figured out a way for her to get together with you." Cathy turned a calculating smile on Grey. "I lied about meeting a good friend of yours, who I said was going to fix the two of you up for a second chance. It sounded lame, but it was the best I could do last-minute."

Rally picked his nails.

"Having checked out the area around your house, I knew there was an access road to the pond that backed up to your property. Luckily for me, it was a vacation home, and I could come and go as I pleased. I lured Mindy along, telling her that I'd planned a picnic for the two of you. I even brought props—a basket and blanket. I talked her into setting up everything next to the water, knowing she couldn't swim, and pushed her in. Poor thing freaked out and fought it and went under fast."

I grimaced.

"I couldn't believe my luck when she washed up on your side." Cathy tittered.

"The sound effects are annoying." Rally hit the side of his head and laughed.

Grey's jaw was locked so hard, his teeth must hurt.

"If you think about it, it was a just end, considering everything I had to listen to, and I shouldn't be punished further."

Cathy's narcissistic rambling was coming to an end, and Grey and I needed to get the upper hand against two people with guns who were just itching to pull the trigger. I wasn't sure if Grey was carrying, but drawing his gun wouldn't go unnoticed. We needed a diversion.

"Help me understand," Grey said in a placating tone. "The case has been pushed to the bottom of the stack, and to my knowledge, no one ever looked at you as a suspect, so what's this all about?"

"Because it's fun." *Duh* in Cathy's tone. "And personal. It's your own fault. After all I heard, I decided I wanted a relationship with you, which would've been impossible with Mindy alive."

"I don't remember ever meeting you." Grey appeared to be searching his memory.

"That's because you wouldn't give me the time of day. Better than me, were you?" Cathy asked in a snotty tone. "I tried a couple of different looks… but you were sucked into yourself and abrasive to my attempts. Mindy had terrible taste in men; should've known you'd be a jerk."

"When?" Grey barked.

"Once you were a person of interest, I started following you around. If you hadn't been such a jerk…" Her eyes skirted to me for a half-second. "I clearly wasn't your type. Who'd guess it'd be dowdy and not very bright?"

Grey scrutinized her as though she were a specimen under a microscope.

"I wanted to wipe the smirk off your face permanently. Rally talked me down, saying that it was better if I didn't do it myself, pointing out that I lacked cred. He knew someone who knew someone. When I heard a million dollars, I figured back to square one." Cathy shot a sideways glance at Rally, who remained unemotional. "See how that turned out?" She pointed the muzzle of the gun at Grey's chest.

"Where's your connection now?" Grey asked.

"The man who supplied the number is in prison." Rally snorted.

"You used the information anyway?" Grey asked, his tone letting Rally know he stupid he was.

Rally glared.

No way Cathy shelled out the money. I'd done a background check on her, and neither she nor her family had the zeros in their bank account.

"You didn't get your money's worth, did you?" Grey half-laughed, not one bit amused.

Rally had the money. Millions in his trust fund. His family had even more should he run out. But why would he get involved? He was stupid, but was he *that* stupid? Cathy's accomplice, maybe? "You're part of all this craziness?" I asked him. I wanted to say, *Millions at your disposal was too boring, so you decided to blow it on felonies?* but refrained.

"It was supposed to be a short-term loan. That didn't go as planned." Cathy sent Rally an apologetic look. "He's always been there to help me hone one of my plans and keep me on track so I don't go off half-cocked. Always stressing patience."

"We were meant for each other." Rally smiled at Cathy. "Once the playing field was cleared, there was nothing to stand in the way of us being together." Rally turned to me. "You appeared on the scene out of nowhere. I saw through your writer con, knowing it was all bull—you're not smart enough to put together a sentence. A background check turned up nothing. It was tedious tracking you down, tailing you; you're a bore."

"Now you can get your truck out of storage." Cathy beamed at him.

"You ran me off the road?" Grey turned on Rally. "What the hell for?"

"Because I could," he said with a sneer. "What could you do about it? Nothing."

"I guess you're disappointed we lived?" I asked.

"Maybe at first." Cathy grinned. "Then Rally met you and wanted a hookup, and when you ignored his come-ons and made it clear no way, boy did he jump grumpy." She turned to him. "But I soothed your hurt feelings, didn't I, honey bunny?"

A barfing noise seemed appropriate, but I contained myself. Just barely.

Rally smiled at Cathy in a calculating way. It would creep me out. Not her. She graced him with a moony smile.

"You thought I was stupid," Rally said to me. "Big mistake. I knew your meeting with Detective Donnelly was a setup to see if I'd follow you. Joke was on you; Cathy was already in place, snapping pictures. It didn't take long after that to figure out that I'd been hosed out of a lot of money."

I let out a thankful sigh. At least he didn't seem to know that he'd been dealing with me all along and instead still thought he'd spoken with my father, whose identity he didn't seem to know. It didn't answer the question of why he thought my dad was a hitman. Or knew how to hire one.

"If you're the perpetrator of all things wrong in Mindy's life, why would she have kept a journal detailing her crimes?" Grey asked.

"We came up with the idea, along with the plan to pitch it to an agent that I met at one of the Charles's barbeques; the man bragged he was always looking for material." Cathy smiled at Grey, who clenched his jaw again. "I wrote several parts of it, doing my best to imitate her style. Always wondered if it would pass a handwriting analysis, but as far as I know, no one ever had it done."

"This has all been a game to you?" I asked, horrified. "And all because Grey wouldn't give you the time of day?"

Cathy shot me a hate glare.

Rally held up his hands. "I had nothing to do with any of this; my hands are clean. I've been an innocent bystander, doing my best to make sure that Cathy doesn't get too worked up over her next wild idea."

Delusional. Paying for the hit made him guilty of attempted murder. Then there was the hit-and-run. Neither Grey nor I commented on that.

Rally's quickness to claim non-involvement left open the question of what else had Cathy done?

"How about a little negotiation?" Grey threw out. "There has to be something you want more than the two of us dead. I'm an ex-cop, as you both know, and can help you cover up any previous felonious activities so you're never found out and neither of you risk going to prison."

"If only I'd been able to stop the money transfer." Rally shot a glare at Cathy, who tittered, then turned to Grey. "You're not stupid… Or maybe you are if you think I'll believe your offer is genuine." He motioned to Cathy. "Let's get out of here. Totally tired of this dump and these people."

Cathy waved her gun around. "Either of you have a coin? We can flip to see which of you dies first."

Chapter Thirty-Two

I'd never stared down death before and was unsure of the protocol but knew that I wasn't going down without a fight. I also knew Grey felt the same way and would fight for us both. I wished I had a minute to formulate a plan with him.

Rally, who hadn't killed anyone, wasn't going to start today, judging from his casual stance. But Cathy had apparently done a mental coin toss and now locked her sights on Grey, a maniacal grin on her face.

I could taste my fear and feel the adrenaline rush and struggled to keep myself under control. I'd already nixed begging for my life, knowing that tactic would only end up entertaining them. I mentally assigned Grey to Cathy and myself to Rally, since he was the closer of the two. If I wasn't getting out alive, then neither was he, no matter what I had to do.

On three, I told myself. One… I leapt at Rally at the same moment Grey hurled himself at Cathy. I wrapped myself around his lower legs, and he hit the ground with a satisfying groan. I leapt to my feet, evaded his attempt to grab my skirt, and planted my foot on his throat.

A gunshot went off.

The door burst open. From the sound of it, it had almost been kicked off the hinges.

Another gunshot.

Cathy's scream reverberated around the room.

Rally had wrapped his hand around one of my ankles but let it drop away without a struggle.

I looked up into my dad's grinning face. He was pressing the muzzle of his gun to the middle of Rally's forehead, Seven behind him.

Cathy screamed again, this time in frustration. The woman attempted to reach for her gun, but Grey—who'd knocked the gun out of her hand, causing it to discharge—kicked it out of her reach.

"Don't think so," he barked.

"There's a pair of handcuffs on that chair." I pointed.

Seven unlocked the cuffs and tossed them to Grey, who handcuffed her and left her sitting on the floor.

Dad leaned down, fisted Rally's shirt, and lifted him to his feet in one swift move. He spun him around and shoved his face into the wall, then took off his belt and used it to secure his hands. Then he pushed him to his knees.

"You're all going to die," Cathy screeched, then unleashed a litany of every filthy word she could come up with.

"Shut up," Rally roared. "Not another word

until my lawyer shows up."

I launched myself at my dad, who caught me, wrapping his arms around me. "You're in so much trouble, mister," I whispered. "I love you, missed you, and where the hell have you been?"

"You listen to me, missy…" He leaned down and laid a big smacking kiss on my cheek. "Love you back. Your old man is retiring, so I'm going to be underfoot more. Plenty of time to share stories later." He looked to Seven. "When are your friends getting here?"

The door ricocheted off the wall again. To its credit, it wasn't showing signs of the beating it'd taken this morning. Miami's finest filled the doorway, guns drawn. Seven nodded at one, then approached the officers and did all the talking.

Grey came over and enveloped me in a hard hug, then laid a big kiss on me. "Don't you go anywhere without me," he ordered. I grinned at him and made a quick introduction to my dad, Edgar Finn.

My dad, whose eyebrows were up in his hairline, backed me into a corner, keeping his arm around me. "Who was that manhandling my daughter?"

"It's a long story." I gave him a goofy smile.

"Whoever that is has to get my okay or he can hit the road," Dad grouched as he scanned the room. "What the hell happened to my office?"

"It's clean, for one thing," I grouched back.

"I've missed you." Dad wrapped his arms around me in a long, tight hug.

"Same here."

We turned to face the room as more cops arrived. We'd missed Rally being put in cuffs. Both he and Cathy were being read their rights.

"I'm Rally Charles III, and I demand to call my lawyer." If that was meant to impress the cops, big fail.

They were led out, Cathy screeching her head off.

Grey and Seven were surrounded by several cops, and they had a short conversation with plenty of hand-waving.

A cop came over and asked us to go downstairs. On the way down, Dad whispered, "Answer all their questions truthfully. Keep it short and to the point."

I nodded and walked down the stairs, my dad behind me, and the two of us walked over to my SUV. I was happy to be out in the fresh air.

"I'll be right back." Dad patted my shoulder.

Rally and Cathy had been loaded into the backs of separate cop cars, which now pulled out. A young, hottie cop came over to question me. I told him everything that had happened today, starting with the phone call from Avery.

Grey, Seven, and my dad were getting more of an interrogation, and I was happy to be left out. I was still a jittery mess over facing death and hoping it never happened again.

Avery came rushing out of the building and hugged me hard. "What the heck?" She stepped back and checked me out from head to toe. "I was going upstairs for a chat and ran into Grey. He told me to go back to my office, lock the door, and take cover. I was sorry to miss the action, but when I heard gunshots, not so much."

"My dad's back." I smiled and pointed.

"Bet he's got a good story, and I don't want to miss a word of it." Avery poked me in the side as Dad and Grey walked over. "I call dibs on telling Rella what went down here today."

"I see you two have had time to talk," I said to my dad.

"This young man says you have something to tell me," Dad said in a teasing tone.

Really?

Grey smirked.

"This is my, uh…"

"Boyfriend," Grey whispered.

"And they live together," Avery announced.

My cheeks burned.

"When are you two getting married?" Dad's eyes narrowed on Grey.

"Daddy, please."

"I'm putting in an order for a couple of grandkids, and if Gram knows you're a… living together, she's probably already done it, along with setting the date." Dad gave Grey and me a stern look. "When I got called out of town, you two weren't… I can't wait to hear how you met."

I hurriedly smacked Avery, in case she was preparing to blurt out the details.

Not one to miss anything, Dad said, "Bet it's a good one."

Chapter Thirty-Three

Rella had invited everyone over to her condo at mid-morning the next day. Only the fact that she'd hired the chef from the Cat House to cook had convinced me to get out of bed in time to go.

Yesterday had been a long day. Our presence had been requested at the police station, and Avery had been disappointed she wasn't included. It was my first trip there, and I didn't need to go back. Ever. The officers were nice, but… people were locked up somewhere out of sight. We'd been separated and questioned and questioned again. Finally, they seemed satisfied, and we got to walk out with the admonition not to leave town.

Turned out, Cathy completely flipped her switch on the way to the station and ended up getting a ride to the hospital for a mental health check to see if she was faking or not. Rally pled his innocence to anyone who would listen, telling them he was there to stop Cathy and had nothing to do with any of her crimes. He'd been booked and was currently awaiting a date with a judge to tell his story.

My dad and I were the first to be released, and Rella and Avery waiting in the parking lot were a welcome sight. Dad and I got into Rella's car for the ride home, while Avery waited in her car for the guys to be released. It was a silent drive home. I sat practically on top of my dad, not wanting to let him out of my sight.

We all rode up to the top floor together and said good-bye to Rella, who informed us about the breakfast she'd planned at her place in the morning.

"So much to talk about," I said once the door closed. "Drink?" Dad nodded, and we went into the kitchen, got drinks, and sat in the living room.

"I really like Grey," Dad said. "Solid guy. You chose well."

I told him the whole story—how I'd snooped through his office and ended up kidnapping Grey. I didn't gloss over anything I'd done.

Dad laughed for a good five minutes. "You really are my daughter." He enveloped me in a hug.

"I owe you an apology for the invasion of your privacy, but if I hadn't done it, Grey would be dead, so not too sorry. And now, mister, about that office of yours... Insurance salesman?" I rolled my eyes. "I'm certain you've never sold a policy in your life. Homeowners or some such, wasn't it?"

"You know very well it was a one-stop shop." Dad laughed.

"What were you really doing?"

"What I can tell you is that I worked undercover for the FBI and helped bring down bad guys in a variety of ways. I established a reputation in criminal circles as being up for anything as long as the price was right. It came as a shock, to my clients anyway, that every one of them ended up in prison. Based on the number Rally called, the criminal he got it from had wanted the same service and is now locked up. It would be interesting to know what the relationship is between the two men. That's all I can say, as I took an oath to keep my trap shut. That applies even after I've left service."

"Am I in legal trouble, having used government resources?"

"Your old man is going to take care of this situation. I've still got connections in the bureau, and once they hear the whole story, they're going to set their sights on Rally. Like me, they'll have a few questions for him."

I hugged him hard. "If something had happened and you'd been killed, would they have notified me?" I shuddered at the thought of never knowing.

He hesitated for so long, I already knew the answer. "Probably not immediately, but eventually, yes. But I'm back and not going anywhere. You'll have me around to tell you what to do for a long time to come."

Grey walked in and pulled me into his arms, hugging me.

"I'll see you two at breakfast." Dad slipped out quietly.

* * *

Rella had set the table out on the balcony and told me to invite the need-to-know people. Dad arrived with Seven. Not sure how they met. The latter singled Avery out to flirt with, and she informed him he was a hot lug but not her type. He laughed.

I'd been chosen as door-greeter. "What are you doing here?" I asked Ender upon opening the door. He ignored me, busy tugging on Gram's arm.

"Really, Harper, you're being rude." Gram tsked, pulling away and shoving Ender inside (with his help). He grinned at her.

"Lucky me, I showed up when Gram was getting ready to jet out the door, and once I heard the details, I invited myself." Ender continued to grin. "Very opportune, I'd say."

It was an amazingly gorgeous day to have breakfast outside on the balcony, the sun glittering off the blue water below and a family-and-friends affair around the table. The cook fixed us each one of his signature waffle stacks, and the food was quickly devoured, Ender the only one to eat two.

"If you barf," I said, "do it in your shoe and try not to make a mess."

Most laughed.

Gram shook her head and finger at me and poked Ender. "No barfing." He grinned back at her.

When everyone was finished and the plates cleared away, Rella refilled drinks and had us all move down to the other end of the balcony to sit in the deck chairs, each with its own footrest.

"How is it that Dad and Seven were the ones to burst through the doors... ahead of the cops, I might add?" I asked.

"Your phone call had us both flying in your direction, albeit separately," Seven said. "Grey and I had already concluded our business, and he was headed home when he got your call. I was en route to another appointment when I got Grey's call and U-turned. On the way to your office, I called a law enforcement friend who'd already been consulting with me and Grey, and he said reinforcements were on the way. I'm perusing the parking lot when this old man practically sideswipes me, backing me up so that he can hog two parking places, which I contend is laziness, even if it turns out he owns the building."

"Seven ordered me to come back another time, thinking I'd cower in my trainers, and I laughed.

Told him mine are bigger than yours any day of the week." Dad smirked.

Everyone laughed.

Rella and I blushed.

"When he introduced himself as Old Man Finn, I made the connection to crazy chick and filled him in, telling him he might want to stay in his car," Seven said.

Dad snorted. "Seven's idea of filling me in was half-assed at best. Upon hearing my daughter might be in trouble, no way was I waiting. Told him if he was a 'fraidy, he could be the one to wait in the parking lot. Whipped open my jacket and drew my firearm, saying, 'Follow me, son.'" He demonstrated.

Grey laughed.

I shook my head.

"Call me 'fraidy and see what happens," Ender taunted with a grin.

"I heard you don't have a girlfriend," Gram said to Seven. "I'm available." She winked at him.

"You're too old for him," Dad pointed out.

"Can't blame a girl for trying."

I shot Seven an "I told you so" look.

"I've got a couple of updates," he said. "Cathy was Baker-acted, so she's in the looney bin until a court decides otherwise. Rally's awaiting a bail hearing. I'm sure his father will throw his weight around to get him released."

"If that happens, let me know. I don't want him showing back up at the office without some warning," Grey said.

I held up my hand. "I want all of you to know I'm removing my nose from Grey's business and concentrating on my own. I've had enough excitement."

Grey wrapped his arm around me.

"I'm always the boring one." Rella sighed.

"Anyone ever tells you that to your face, you tell me." Avery air-boxed.

"Staring down the barrel of a gun is not fun," I said. "Especially when you know the person on the other end is going to pull the trigger." My friends and I grimaced. "I'm looking forward to a little boring."

~*~

*PREVIEW THE NEXT IN
THE SERIES*

NOT GUILTY

*When you're being framed for murder,
should you draw a line in the sand...
or run for the water?*

Chapter One

"Avery English, when are you going to start locking your door?" Seven demanded in a grouchy tone as he kicked open the door and crossed the threshold, a paper cup in each hand.

I wiped the smirk off my face as I turned and faced the blond-haired, blue-eyed hottie dressed in jeans and a dress shirt. Little did Seven Donnelly know, but his latest acquisition—a black Escalade with tinted windows—had caught my attention when it passed by on the large security monitor that sat on the corner of my desk. I'd tracked the car as it curved around the back of the building and pulled into the underground garage. He also didn't need to know that I knew exactly how long it would take him to climb the stairs to the second floor.

"Would you believe that a client just left?" I took off my oversized cat-shaped glasses and tossed them in the drawer, knowing that he didn't like them. I didn't actually need glasses, but they lent credence to the nerdy persona I liked to project. He claimed they blocked his ability to see my "beautiful" eyes.

With a shove, Seven slammed the door shut and strutted over to my desk like he owned the place. He set down a cup of coffee right under my nose like he did every morning on the way to his third-floor office.

I'd really begun to look forward to these visits.

The previous occupant of the third floor and owner of the property had recently retired and now spent most of his time with cronies on the golf course, showing up on occasion to make sure the building was still standing. Seven had partnered with his longtime friend Grey West, both ex-cops, in their newly formed security firm, WD Consulting, which had moved into the space vacated by the owner.

"I think you just made that up so you don't have to listen to another safety lecture." He gave me a piercing stare, one hand reaching out and pushing back a couple stray locks of my sun-streaked hair that had come loose from the messy twist I'd fashioned earlier. He stepped back, claimed one of the two chairs in front of my desk, and stretched his legs out. Settling back, he raised his cup and winked. "I happen to know you're obsessive about detail, so were you by chance expecting me?" He cut off my response with a wave of his hand. "I know what's coming next—you're going to tell me that another client's about to walk through the door. Do I have that right? No answer needed, as I know how accommodating you are to your clients—meeting most of them on their turf—hence only a handful grace these premises. Good excuse, though. Save it for someone who doesn't know you."

"Did you hear that?" I tilted my head, staring up at the ceiling. "Grey's yelling for you to get upstairs and get some work done."

Stupid grin on his face, Seven rolled his eyes. "With this building's layers of concrete, we could have a bloody free-for-all going on up there and you'd never hear a thing."

"That's all we need." I air-boxed.

"How about dinner? Say yes. I promise you won't regret it."

"I don't date." Rarely anyway. I'd done my share of casual encounters and friend fix-ups, and they'd turned out okay, but nothing special. After a lot of stilted conversations where I'd done my best to dumb it down, they always ended on an awkward note with my date as eager for the evening to come to an end as I was.

"That's a new excuse. You're usually busy, with some client demanding your attention." He gave me an exaggerated frown.

It was hard not to laugh, and it just slipped out. I'd done my best to discourage him, hadn't I? He was just so damn cute, but I wasn't going to go into all the ways that we were better off being casual friends. "The truth is, I don't date clients." Actually, I liked the friendly banter and didn't want it to change.

"When it comes to WD's finances, you deal primarily with Grey. You're thinking too hard." Seven's feet hit the floor, and he leaned forward. "One dinner, no expectations." He crooked his head to the side and stared at the security monitor. "We need a couple of these upstairs. In the meantime, something's going on…"

My eyes shot to the monitor. "What's happening?"

Seven and I watched as another Miami-Dade police car followed the first one into the parking lot and both parked in front of the building. The officers got out, checked out the building and exchanged a few words, then headed to the entrance.

"They buzzed me." I eyed the intercom pad at the door. "Wonder if they just started pushing buttons to see who might answer."

"This probably isn't a social call." Seven stood.

"I'll go down and find out what's going on."

I ignored the shiver that raced up my spine. Or tried to, anyway. "Be careful. I know you used to be one of them, but you never know."

"I knew you liked me." He grinned and raised his shirt, showing off impeccable abs as well as the gun holstered at his waist. "In case you need peace of mind, I've got backup on the off chance I need it. In this case, I highly doubt it will be necessary."

I gave him a weak smile.

Seven crossed to the door and double-checked the lock, then turned back to me. "Keep it locked until I get back."

"You don't have to tell me twice." I saluted as he shut the door. I thought of Hugo's cleaning service on the first floor and hoped that none of the guys that worked for him were in any kind of trouble.

~*~

Other Titles by Deborah Brown

BISCAYNE BAY SERIES
Hired Killer
Not Guilty (September 2021)
Jilted (October 2021)

PARADISE SERIES
Crazy in Paradise
Deception in Paradise
Trouble in Paradise
Murder in Paradise
Greed in Paradise
Revenge in Paradise
Kidnapped in Paradise
Swindled in Paradise
Executed in Paradise
Hurricane in Paradise
Lottery in Paradise
Ambushed in Paradise
Christmas in Paradise
Blownup in Paradise
Psycho in Paradise
Overdose in Paradise
Initiation in Paradise
Jealous in Paradise
Wronged in Paradise
Vanished in Paradise
Fraud in Paradise
Naive in Paradise
Bodies in Paradise
Accused in Paradise

Deborah's books are available on Amazon
amazon.com/Deborah-Brown/e/B0059MAIKQ

About the Author

Deborah Brown is an Amazon bestselling author of the Paradise series. She lives on the Gulf of Mexico, with her ungrateful animals, where Mother Nature takes out her bad attitude in the form of hurricanes.

For a free short story, sign up for my newsletter. It will also keep you up-to-date with new releases and special promotions: www.deborahbrownbooks.com

Follow on FaceBook: facebook.com/DeborahBrownAuthor

You can contact her at Wildcurls@hotmail.com

Deborah's books are available on Amazon

amazon.com/Deborah-Brown/e/B0059MAIKQ

Made in the USA
Coppell, TX
24 August 2021

61108350R00177